Dead
on the
DOCK

Beth Everett

For information contact www.beth-everett.com

Cover illustration © 2015 Edel Rodriguez

Cover Design by Maggie Olson
Lyric from "Hercules" by Guster reprinted by permission.

ISBN-13: 9780692681220
ISBN-10: 0692681221
LCCN: 2016904532

Beth Fernandez, Portland, Oregon

for Bev and Bob, who taught me to be brave

DEAD ON THE DOCK

Beth Everett

THE NIGHT SKY WAS WILD with stars. The moon hung over the mountaintop in a shy sliver, and the black lake replied to the sky in mirrored tribute. Johnson Camp glowed from across the lake. Emily wondered who was sleeping in the cabin where she'd spent the last fifteen summers. Did they count the knots in the pine on the ceiling as they fell asleep, as she had? Were they comfortable in her bed?

Nine forty-five. Time to go. She slipped her bony feet into the cheap rubber flip-flops that sat by the door and headed outside, careful not to let the cabin's screen door slam behind her. She considered letting her eyes adjust to the darkness but decided it was more prudent to turn on her headlamp. The cone-shaped light attracted tiny ghost gnats and exposed a slight mist in the air.

As she crossed the narrow road and found the trail that led to the water's edge, Emily imagined herself the heroine in a novel—romantic and adventurous. Her ratty robe was a flowing cape, her long nightshirt a silk gown. She was admired, longed for, loved. It was these thoughts that gave her wobbly legs the courage to continue.

The branchy woman arrived at the water's edge where she carefully walked the ramp that connected land to dock. It tilted and splashed, reminding her of the lazy man responsible for repairing it. His lack of discipline was what bothered her most. No one should be on the dock until the ramp was properly secured. She would bring it up tomorrow.

"Why are you doing this?" asked an angry voice from behind her.

Emily spun around. "You surprised me! Are you trying to give me a heart attack?" she asked in her most indignant voice, tightening her robe and quickly waving a hand in front of her chest as if it would slow her heartbeat.

She instantly regretted her acerbic response. She should have been kinder. *I take it back. I'm sorry.* The words wouldn't come. What came instead was a guttural bellow as she was pushed backward into the metal boat rack and ricocheted onto the floating dock, her skinny limbs flailing out into the air.

The quick splash of the water as her companion stepped off the dock—a final reminder of the incompetence of others—was the last sound Emily heard before she became one with the darkness that surrounded her.

No birds scattered, no fish dashed from danger. The stars partied on. The moon was caught in its own drama, hoping to borrow more of the sun's light again tomorrow.

CHAPTER 1

Three Days Earlier

IF I WERE A BOAT, I would be a canoe—stable, with the ability to carry burdens for long distances, an ancient design with the capacity to handle rapids without cracking, silent and sleek and one with nature. A canoe cannot be rushed. Whenever I paddle onto a quiet misty lake, I find peace within moments. With every stroke into the glassy water, my troubles fall away.

When my husband and I first started paddling, we used to haul our heavy secondhand Grumman from lake to lake. Then we found a canoe club on Lake Montego in New York, about an hour from our home in suburban New Jersey. The four-hundred-acre lake was in a park with more than a dozen other lakes, so we often had Montego to ourselves. If we did pass another paddler, a nod of hello would be shared or a mention of the beautiful morning or maybe a tip about where a blue heron was sighted.

When our boys were little, Jack and I would steer while the kids sat on cushions in the center of the boat. Their small hands would hang over and drag in the water as we meandered around the edge of the lake, spotting turtles and fish, sometimes quietly watching a deer drink from the shore. For the last eight years, our summers were made up of slow camp memories and long burning fires.

As the boys got older, canoeing became monotonous for them. Jack taught them how to kayak instead, and soon they were racing across the lake to pick blueberries on the rocky island in the east cove, purposely tipping their crafts so they could swim, then darting off on another adventure.

They get the speed gene from their father, who comes from a long line of driven, pedigreed men: his father played polo for Harvard and went on to run his own private equity firm; his grandfather invented a patented part for the steam engine.

If I am a canoe, Jack is a kayak. He prefers a race to a quiet stroll. There is always somewhere to go, something to accomplish, and usually at a speed that blurs my vision. Our boys are teenagers now, and it no longer feels like Jack and I are paddling side by side. I'm on the water's edge picking blueberries, and he has us competing in a race that I don't want to win.

I used to have my own dreams. When Jack and I met sixteen years ago, I'd just finished an undergraduate degree in economics and was about to join the Peace Corps. My world was full of Nobel Prize winners who argued with each other about the best way to save the world from financial ruin. But then I met Jack and became a supporter of his dreams instead of the architect of my own. We built a family as Jack and Lee Morgan, and I somehow lost Lee Harding in the construction process.

Economic theory was replaced with vaccine appointments and nightly readings of Dr. Seuss. I became secretary of the PTA instead of director of an NGO. All my decisions were made around my children. Looking back, I can see that I created a family to replace the one I'd lost so early in life—I was ten years old when I found my mother dead from an aneurism, just two years after my father passed away from cancer. The trauma of my childhood is something I still carry with me.

Jack wasn't impressed by my overconsumption of motherhood, however. He fell into trouble with a woman he worked with while I was pregnant with our second child. She had a boob job and laughed at his jokes. She knew how long a trade took to clear and had a subscription to the *Wall Street Journal*. She didn't have to be anywhere, and she didn't ignore him to take care of someone else.

My boobs, on the other hand, were tired and so was I—though not so tired that I couldn't figure out what was going on. I packed Jack's bags and notified his mother he'd be coming. But when he fell to his knees, crying on my swollen belly, I let him stay. I had always imagined I wouldn't be "that" woman, the one who took her cheating husband back, but fear and exhaustion aided my decision.

It took a long time for us to recover. For the first few years, I believed I had only stayed for my children, but as the kids grew older, I realized there was real love between the two of us. Jack had earned my respect back by becoming a completely dedicated father and husband.

While on a two-week trip back to my hometown of San Francisco last winter, I'd come dangerously close to a betrayal of my own. I returned home with the realization that I was responsible for my own happiness. It was so cliché, but I really needed to find out who I was, separately from motherhood and marriage. So I signed up for a GRE study course and aced the test. I was accepted at Columbia University's School of International and Public Affairs, and I just finished the first year of my master's degree in Global Affairs.

Jack and I talked a lot about what I wanted to do post-graduation. I knew that my heart belonged to the extreme poor; I was determined to help the world's bottom billion. Many of the jobs that interested me required working overseas, and the idea of taking our kids abroad to see the world and learn about how others lived excited me. I felt that living in Central America or Africa would provide our privileged boys with an education unlike any other, and I nurtured a fantasy that my kids would invent water filtration systems that saved lives or find a cure for Tuberculosis.

This was not Jack's dream. He didn't plan on retiring from his job early to join me in fighting diseases among the poor in Haiti or in any other place without running water. He preferred to send a check. According to him, the only thing our kids would get out of living in Africa would be exposure to Malaria.

This is how it happens. This is how people grow apart. I'd always figured one of us would die or Jack would go through a midlife crisis and trade me in for a twenty-something intern. It never occurred to me that we would argue over our dreams. Maybe the difference had always been there.

Jack is a kayak. I am a canoe.

CHAPTER 2

THE HOUSE WAS SADLY QUIET on the Monday morning that I left. We had dropped the boys off the day before at the upstate summer camp they had attended for several years in a row. Jack Jr. was sixteen and had graduated to the Junior Counselor Program, which annoyed his fourteen-year-old brother, Max, to no end. I would not see my kids again for two weeks, which was when the camp held their Visitation Day.

The ride back from upstate New York had been long and quiet. We both knew that the divide between us was widening, but neither of us had a solution. We were talked out. I didn't want drama, so I hired a dog sitter and ran away to our lake camp on Lake Montego.

I sent my husband a text. *I need some time to myself. Please respect that. I will call you during the week.* It wasn't the most courteous way to tell your husband you were going away, but I didn't feel like arguing about issues that couldn't be resolved with words.

The loft in our barn had its own summer goods corner. I began to gather the usual family items, like an old rusty tin of vintage game pieces and a sack of life jackets, before remembering I would be on my own. Instead I grabbed my own life jacket and my two favorite wooden paddles, which were mixed into a stack of high-tech carbon ones that belonged to Jack and the boys. One was an antique, the other carved by myself at a paddle-making workshop I'd gone to years ago. I loaded one bin with kitchen supplies and another bin with Pendleton blankets, a quilt, and throw pillows that had "Lake" and "New York" stitched onto their surface in a campy style. I looked around the loft at the assorted equipment, much of it outdated: a long abandoned tricycle, a once-loved puppet theatre, and other pieces of my kids' younger years that I didn't have the heart to get rid of. The emotions of loss and love welled up, but I pushed them back down and locked the musty old space before getting into my half-stuffed car.

The drive to Lake Montego took just short of an hour. The closer I got to camp, the faster I found myself driving. We'd been going to the lake for eight years but hadn't had a lot of time to come that year because of a big deal Jack was working on.

I spotted a tall skinny backpacker trudging up the park road about two miles before the camp turnoff. He had hair like Buckwheat, part Afro, part dreadlocks. It came together in a chaos that made him instantly recognizable. I pulled over.

"Freddie!" I called out.

"Lee!" Freddie Papius cried when he recognized me. His smile was like the summer sun, generous and warm on the soul. He was dressed head to toe in lightweight waterproof gear. His thin limbs were tight with muscle. He didn't own a car and thought nothing of walking the five miles uphill from the bus stop on the highway to the camp, while carrying an enormous pack, before hopping in a boat and paddling for the rest of the night. I'd seen how he'd done it—feeding his twiggy body with enough food to satisfy three grown men. Anyone who'd invited him to dinner at camp knew to buy plenty of food to grill first.

"Let me give you a lift," I said, pushing the passenger door open for him.

He hesitated at first, but threw his backpack in the rear seat and hopped in.

I drove the winding road as he told me how the past year had gone. His faded accent originated from the Caribbean, but Freddie was a New Yorker now, living in Brooklyn and etching out a life as a techie, only taking contract work so he could spend long periods of time at the lake during the summer months.

Freddie was the camp sage. There was a calm in him that was both intimidating and enviable. When he wasn't working in computers, he spent most of his time teaching the elusive skill of serenity at a lower Manhattan meditation center. I went to one of his classes once. It was impossible for me to sit still that long. I'd spent the hour shifting on my rolled blanket and trying not to giggle. Here at camp, he could always be found helping with whatever project was being constructed or repaired but never staying afterwards for the cold beer and the guy talk. He was a lone paddler, pursuing solitude at sunrise and sunset. He was rarely seen in between.

When I turned onto the unmarked camp road, he jumped out and released the metal cable that blocked the entrance. The narrow, crumbling road that led to camp cut through dense forest and rocky terrain. I stopped the car when Freddie spotted two young fawns munching grass in the woods.

"Hello, beautiful," I whispered as they went dashing back into the shrub.

Sunlight made its way into the forest in specks and spots, just enough to highlight the mossy rocks and lacy branches of the woods. I grew up in San Francisco. I'd always camped in the fern-filled forests of the giant coastal redwood trees. It took a while for me to fall for the rocky terrain and sticklike trees of upstate New York. I called these "skinny woods."

Down the steep hill I could see the first views of the lake with the sun reflecting in tiny sapphire lights. A short time later, a "Private Property" sign announced our arrival in camp. It was actually public land—New York State Parks—but the sign was meant to keep the masses out. An aristocracy of old people ran Camp Montego; members whose parents had been among the first to sleep in the cabins felt they owned the place. Their goal was to keep it small, and it had worked. Even after coming for the past eight summers, Jack and I were among a small number of renters. One had to try very hard to find membership paperwork and maneuver around the red tape to become a member.

The CCC, the Civilian Conservation Corps, had built Camp Montego and many similar camps during the great depression when destitute men left their families to build our country's park system. They were provided with food, clothing, shelter, and a small stipend for their work. The camps were intended as retreats for middle management in the heyday of the American corporation, and Montego had originally been leased by a Manhattan-based men's luxury clothing company. But the CCC disappeared after the start of World War II, the chestnut trees that had been used to build the compound were long gone due to blight, and the men's clothing store couldn't survive casual Friday. Camp Montego now owned the lease.

A rustic-style pavilion sat on the hilltop at the tip of the peninsula and served as the heart of the camp. Debarked logs served as railings for a wraparound porch lined with Adirondack chairs. A grand stone fireplace was the centerpiece of the building, its stacked boulders seeming to hold the structure in place. Long-abandoned hand-crafted canoes hung from the ceiling. I could imagine the men who'd built them lovingly sanding and polishing the sleek shapes. They were beautiful but heavy compared to today's Kevlar version, and thus served as decorations.

The camp was dead quiet, as it usually was on weekdays, even in the middle of July. We had already reserved the cabin for the following weekend, so it was mine through Sunday. I pulled into a parking space on the gravel lot. The lake was visible on both sides of the peninsula. Cabins spotted the hillside toward the water's edge. The compact, two- and three-room huts had million-dollar views from inside, which overlooked the silent waters and dense shrubby shoreline.

A woman emerged from a little cabin on the hill above the parking lot. Like Freddie, Luanne Murphy was a scrappy Brooklynite. She never stopped moving, so although her five-foot-two frame was as thin as a birch tree, it was pure muscle. She could out-paddle the strongest of men and out-swim a dolphin. I'd rarely seen her wear anything other than a swimsuit or shorts and a sports tank. She had no time for beauty products. Her brown hair was usually pulled from her tan Roman face with a rubber band. Her only cosmetic was zinc.

I loved all of my summer friends, but Luanne was definitely my favorite. She was camp supervisor—collecting fees and making sure people left their boats in the right spots. Luanne was both dictator and bodyguard. She'd been known to chase raccoons, bears, and trespassers out of the camp. I once saw her break up a fight between two huge guys in the parking lot. She fearlessly placed herself right in between them and commanded them to "knock it off." They'd both backed down.

Get on her bad side, as many in the camp had, and you'd walk around the lakeshore through tick-infested brush to avoid her. I had learned early on to check in, pay my fees, and not go past the ropes at the swim dock. We'd always gotten along just fine. Luanne's tough city edge was cut with a kindness for those she loved that ran deep. She was the mother of four fantastic, wild girls. They grew up summering here but had begun to abandon their boats for boys and college. Her husband, Patrick, was a bartender in Brooklyn who traveled up to camp on the weekends from Memorial Day to Labor Day.

"Leeeee!" Luanne rushed down the hill and gave me a bone-breaking hug. "Where is everybody?" she asked and then threw in, "Hey, Freddie," as if she had seen him yesterday, which she may have. Freddie waved and disappeared into a bunkhouse called Sycamore. All of the cabins were named after trees.

"I'm alone this time, Luanne." This had been fine until I said the words. Then a wave of emotion came at me.

"What's goin' on? Come on, I'll help you unpack. You want some cawfee?" Luanne's Brooklyn accent was thick—some of her O's were A's and sometimes U's—and she drank more coffee than anyone I'd ever met. She always had a travel mug in her hand.

"Forget the coffee, Luanne. I have bourbon, and I brought white wine for you," I added with a smile. Luanne wasn't an alcohol drinker, unless it was white wine. Even then, two glasses and she was toast.

"Later. Come on." She took the liberty of opening my hatchback and grabbed several bags with her thin but toned arms.

We walked down the hill to Birch, where I usually stayed. Out front, a weather-beaten picnic table and two Adirondack chairs sat on uneven ground, soaking in their million-dollar view. Luanne pushed the unlocked door open and dropped my bags onto the kitchen counter. I walked in and took a deep breath. I loved the smell of the musty cabin. It carried with it decades of dried chestnut and pine. Maybe a little mildew too, but that didn't bother me here.

"I cleaned up the mouse crap on the counters. There is a new canister of gas for the stove," Luanne said as she moved around the room opening curtains and straightening chairs. A five-gallon container of water sat on the counter. Luanne had already hauled it from the well up the road. She never stood still.

"Thanks so much, Lu," I said as I looked around the room of the cabin, reacquainting myself with my home away from home. I set a picnic basket full of goodies on the wooden counter, where it looked right at home. The kitchen had open apple-green-painted shelving, and a small pastel yellow refrigerator and stove. A tiny sink allowed for minimal dishwashing, which I loved.

What had once been castaway furniture, here looked very camp-and-cottage chic. The best part of the room was a black iron five-candle chandelier, original to the cabin. I'd had thoughts of stealing it and replacing it with a fake. No one would have noticed but me. There was also a rustic square dining table with four mismatched chairs, all chipped and worn from long game nights. Two cushioned armchair rockers from the 1940s joined a somewhat out-of-place but necessary futon in the living room. The sofa usually served as the kids' bed. I would cover it with my grandfather's wool blanket and the throw pillows I'd brought along. The boom and rig for a sailboat were stored on the open beams of the ceiling. Honey-colored, knotty pine walls were adorned with old photos of paddlers holding trophies and a wooden sign with a bear silhouette.

I dropped a bag in the bedroom, which was a just large enough for a full-sized iron bed with a bare mattress. Soon I'd be piling layers of ticking stripe sheets and Pendleton blankets on it. Over the bed hung a Hudson River-style painting that I'd always suspected was worth more than anyone imagined. The camp was full of unfound treasures.

Three sides of the building had enormous screened casement windows that ran from the ceiling to chair-rail height, making the cabin feel like a tent. Luanne had opened them for me, and I knew they would stay that way for the length of my trip. The breeze off the lake provided fresh air to the little hut, which was perched diagonally on the hill so that it looked down on the water from both sides of the living quarters. I mentally thanked those Conservation Corps workers as I looked out at the lake.

My canoe rested on a rack of boats close to the water's edge. It was her home while camp was open. Her cardinal-red body clashed beautifully with the brightness of the forest. I felt the excitement of seeing an old friend and couldn't wait to get her on the water.

"I'll leave you to settle in," Luanne said, reading my silence. "Drinks at six?" This was a long-standing tradition with us. Luanne didn't sit still long enough for a cocktail on most nights. I doubted she drank at all when I wasn't here. Our meetings usually resulted in me consuming way too much while her second glass stayed half full.

"Does a cat have an ass?" I replied.

She shook her head and added, "Maddy and Henry Levine are coming up tonight."

"Wonderful!"

"You okay?" she asked casually.

"I'm okay," I lied, but my eyes filled with tears, betraying my words. There was such a deep sense of mourning in my heart, like someone had died. *Something is dying.*

Luanne watched in silence as I busied myself with putting away the groceries.

"I'm going for a paddle," I announced as I wiped my eyes, smiling bravely and shoving the sadness down as far as I could. I'd be fine soon. Everything was better on the lake.

CHAPTER 3

My canoe had missed me.

"Hi, Red," I whispered after making my way down to the boat rack. The stroke of my hand left a mark in the dust of her smooth coat. She was a Kevlar solo canoe and weighed only sixty pounds. When I pulled the boat off the rack and flipped her, a few daddy longlegs scattered frantically. Spiders freaked me out. I felt a pang of guilt as I destroyed their homes with my paddle, but knew I would flip over if one crawled on me while I was out on the water. Reminding myself that the spiders were year-round residents and I was just a seasonal guest helped me be less alarmed—from a distance.

I carried Red on my shoulders to the dock, which was not as easy as I remembered, and finally pushed away from the dock to start my journey with my old companion. We cut through the glassy lake, and I fell into complete peace, my paddle smoothly pushing through the water. We were headed to my favorite swim spot, a white slab of granite that rose from the shore in a cove on the other side of the lake. Taking a quiet dip in an undesignated swim area was my end goal. The big rock in the cove sloped gently into the water, and I could walk on its smooth slope to get in and use it again to get out without stepping in the silty shoreline.

Lake Montego is clean—until a few years ago it was still used as drinking water by the camps—but it's a silt-bottomed lake. I'd grown up swimming in the icy cold waters of Lake Tahoe, where the white sandy bottom meant you knew what you were stepping on. Here, the water was dark with organic debris and the bottom covered in leaves. Eventually, I had overcome my fear of snakes and turtles and imaginary mystery fish that had gone undetected for millions of years, which were coming to eat me, but the unseen had sometimes crept into my imagination like a bad horror movie.

I paddled hard to get to my rock and looked forward to cooling off. Once my boat was secured, I entered the water slowly. Floating on my back, I closed my eyes and drifted into a Zen-like peace. The sadness that had been hanging onto me like moss on a tree departed. I felt nothing, my mind as weightless as my body.

"It's against park rules to swim in undesignated spots!" called a cranky female from the shore. The shrill voice pierced the water. I raised my head to see who was interrupting my time.

A boney woman with wild, white hair that protruded from beneath her nylon sun hat stood on the shoreline. She was wearing a faded denim shirt and nylon hiking pants with a fanny pack protruding from her midsection. A worn backpack was attached to her frail shoulders. She looked more like someone who had escaped the mental hospital than a hiker.

"Thanks for letting me know," I said, pretending to be ignorant of the rules.

I went back to my horizontal position and closed my eyes again, hoping she would go away, but she didn't. Instead she came out of the woods and stood on the rock.

"Two people drowned last summer swimming in undesignated swim areas in the park," she informed me with park ranger-like authority.

I used my hand to shield my eyes from the sun as checked her out. She looked to be in her late sixties and had inquisitive gray eyes.

She noticed my boat. "I can't paddle anymore," she said. "Shoulder injury. I've got a bad back too."

"Sorry to hear that," I finally said.

"We-no-nah Rendezvous," she announced after inspecting Red. "Sixteen-foot touring boat."

"You know your boats."

"Yes. Where do you keep it?" she asked.

I didn't want to be rude, but I also didn't want to tell her my business. I'd gone to the lake to get away, not engage. I was distracted by her pant legs, which were tucked carefully into her long tube socks.

She didn't miss a thing. "Ticks. They're everywhere here. You really have to be careful. I'm a hiker. Hikers know to cover up, especially around the legs."

"Ahh," I said as if I had just learned something.

"Lyme disease is everywhere," she continued as I finally gave up hope that she'd leave and hauled myself out of the water. "The paddlers just don't seem to get that. I see them run around in their shorts and flip-flops everywhere. I tell them, 'You're going to get Lyme disease.'"

"Are you a local?" I asked, trying to turn the tables.

"Me? Oh no. I'm a member of the Montego. It's a canoe club on the lake," she pointed toward camp.

I was surprised, as I knew most of the Montego Club members. "How long have you been a member of Montego?" I asked as I toweled off.

"This is my first summer. I went to Johnson Camp for years, but things are changing over there. Bad management. So I left."

I knew the Johnson family and their camp, which sat on the lake across from Montego. You could see its beach from the dock below my cabin. Like Montego, it had originally been built in the '40s as a summer retreat for city employees. Johnson was all-inclusive; meals, boats, and activities were part of the daily fees. We usually paddled over at least once during our summer trips to visit their dining hall for breakfast, but had skipped it the last few years. The same family had been managing the camp since it was built. Tom Johnson, the grandson of the original manager, was still running it as far as I knew.

"They rented the camp out all summer for a Christian woman's retreat."

"Really?" This surprised me. So many people had been going there year after year. "I guess they must've gotten an offer they couldn't refuse." Times were hard for everyone.

She was watching me intensely, and it made me uncomfortable.

Finally, I pushed my boat into the water and stepped in carefully; every once in a while I still flipped it. I didn't have a dock to hold onto, so it was more awkward than usual, but I was able to paddle off without incident.

"Well, nice talking to you," I said when I was a few feet away.

She looked puzzled by my need to escape her inquisition. She would get her answers soon enough. It would be impossible to avoid her at camp.

I paddled around the corner of the cove, distracted and annoyed that my peaceful swim had been interrupted, and saw two enormous blue herons standing side by side in the shallows before me. We stared at each other for a few precious seconds, but before I could fully appreciate the amazing moment, they took off into the air, their massive wingspans so enormous that I could hear and feel the breeze they created. An involuntary gasp escaped my lips as I watched them fly away.

My first instinct was to call Jack to tell him about the herons... but then I remembered I was here to get away from him. Sadness slowly started creeping in again during my paddle back to camp. I left

Red in the water and tied her to the dock. She looked beautiful on the glassy lake, her reflection softly mimicking her every move.

The cabin had a sort of beautiful loneliness to it, each room with a few of my things scattered here and there. I reached for the 1930s picnic basket I'd brought filled with goodies from home: a bottle of Woodford Reserve Bourbon, a few bottles of wine—and my stash of weed.

I took up marijuana for my headaches and general aches and pains and found that it was great for a lot of other things too, like my obsessively anxious and hyper brain. I don't take any prescription drugs, as I'd had a terrible allergic reaction to anti-inflammatories (my lips had swollen up like a character from the Simpsons, and the doctors told me my throat would be next), and I'd lost all trust in big pharma (I prefer to avoid anything with side effects that include anal leakage or liver failure), but I've been told that the beauty of the calm from cannabis is similar to the effects of Xanax.

After digging through my bags, I found what I was looking for— my trusty bong, a blown glass tube with a little bulbous bottom for holding water and a second, smaller bowl, which I would soon load with bud. I'd purchased it in a hippy store in Woodstock, New York. Jack had tried to hide his distain with a chuckle, but later told me how worried he was that the boys would find it. He always said, "If you have to sneak around to do something, you probably shouldn't do it." I had responded with, "If that's true, then I guess we should stop having sex." That comment had shut him up.

I pulled out a little sticky green bud and picked it apart, loading the broken leaves into the bowl of the pipe. A pungent sweetness filled the air. The view of the lake was before me while I inhaled the smoke from the glass tube, holding it in my lungs for a few seconds before releasing it. I inhaled again until the leaves in the bowl turned to ash.

Soon, my stomach rumbled like an angry dinner bell. Making a single meal was going to be so easy. I'd been a vegetarian my entire life. My parents had been vegetarians, as were my sisters. My husband liked his steak bleeding rare, and my boys took after him, so at home I had to make one carnivorous meal for the guys and another for me. He'd won on that issue. Or I had conceded—like I had on so many issues with the kids. I'd been conceding since the day I decided to stay with him.

I sliced some baby portabellas, onions, and bell peppers and tossed them in olive oil and minced garlic. I placed them on my cast iron grill pan—it was "my" grill pan because everyone in my family knew a piece of meat had never touched it—and headed out to the patio to fire up the barbecue. I stirred the veggies as they sizzled on the pan, sipping a glass of wine and singing and swaying in joyous freedom along to the Decembrists, who played on my portable speakers.

"I smell dinner," I heard over the music.

I looked up to see a large heavyset man with thinning silver hair. His T-shirt worked hard to cover over his vast belly. A pair of tired cargo shorts held on for dear life beneath his bump. He had a kind, weathered face that I imagined had been handsome in his youth. Now he was bloated and grayish.

"Bobby!" I yelled. I set my glass down so I could hug him.

Bobby Richfield was a staple at Montego. His role was camp manager, and like Luanne, he lived here full-time from May through October. He recruited new members, organized races, and ran a two-week paddle training camp for kids each year. He was a handy guy who did most of the maintenance in exchange for the permanent use of one of the cabins.

Bobby had some sort of back injury and was on disability. He walked carefully, and took a daily nap, but his injury didn't keep him from work around camp, though he did recruit the men to help him with heavy lifting. He was the reason the docks got repaired after big storms and the steps down to the swim dock weren't crumbling beneath our feet. He kept busy with daily trips to the lumberyard and hardware store in his old van, and his cabin's patio was always covered in a couple of saw horses and an extension cord for his many electric tools.

"Where's the clan?" he asked.

What was I going to say? No one knew about my marital problems, and I wanted to keep it that way.

"The boys are at camp, and Jack is working on some big deal at work. I came alone," I said in an overly cheery voice. "Can I get you a soda or something?" I asked, knowing he didn't drink alcohol.

"I'm fine, thanks. Just wanted to say hello," he sniffed the air like a bear looking for dinner.

"It's vegetarian, but you're welcome to it," I said, glancing toward the grill. He walked over to take a peek.

"That would be great over a cheese burger," he laughed.

"It's going to be just as good over some mozzarella on a whole wheat bun. Sorry, I didn't bring any burgers, or I would throw one on for you," I said.

"It's okay. Sheila left me a week's worth of dinners in the fridge," he said, backing away from the grill to depart. Bobby's wife Sheila came up on weekends. She was a schoolteacher who took on summer school jobs for extra money.

"Well, thanks for coming by," I said. "I'm so happy to be back up here and see everyone again."

"Yeah, it's pretty great. I go back to the city for a couple of days when I have to, and I'm miserable in the heat and the stench. I'd be here all year if Parks would let me."

This was the down side of the camp not truly belonging to us. You didn't have to pay taxes or a mortgage on a summerhouse that wasn't really yours, but you had to follow the rules made by others. The state park system was very strict about the camp being vacated over the winter. The service road was often impassable in the snow, and falling trees had been known to take out cabins and boat racks.

Bobby always stayed in camp longer than anyone else, though he reported that it got cold fast after Labor Day and the bears would start nosing into the abandoned camp. He'd had some scares with the shaggy scavengers. Once, while he was cooking dinner upstairs, an enormous male broke into the underside of his cabin and ripped the doors clean off of the building. Bobby ran outside banging pots and pans and successfully scared off the two-hundred-fifty-pound beast. The incident may have rattled him, but Bobby wasn't deterred. Those were the dangers of living alone in the woods.

I didn't blame Bobby for wanting to stay. His wife was a bear of a different kind. She had the prissy look of an old schoolhouse marm who'd never gotten laid. During our first years at camp, she'd been there to educate us on the rules at every turn. My kids thought she was some kind of woodland witch. If they did anything wrong, she would suddenly appear to tell them of their sins before seeking me out to repeat herself.

"I found your kids playing at the water tap today," she'd once said.

"Yes, they were filling their water guns," I said, letting her know I was already aware.

"They were splashing and making a muddy mess," she'd replied with a little laugh like she'd found it endearing when it was clear she really hadn't.

"Well, this is why we come up here, for them to get to know the dirt a little better."

Luanne had known Sheila and Bobby for a long time and had a different opinion about their relationship. In her eyes, Sheila was cranky because she was married to Bobby, who had never been as motivated to work at a paying job as he was to work for free in camp. For him, the cabin provision was enough pay. Sheila had been "supporting him and his bad back since they got married." According to Luanne, "Bobby made her a bitch."

Bobby and Luanne had a complicated relationship. Sometimes they were the only two people in camp for days at a time, and they had to get along, but Bobby often overstepped his authority by encouraging campers to break rules. He'd let the Kid's Camp paddlers on the water without life jackets, which sent Luanne through the roof. He would tell people it was okay to bring their dogs to camp, only to have her turn them around and send them home. She felt he liked being the good guy, but in the process, he made her look like a villain.

"That's what he's done to Sheila. The kids love him, but at her expense," Luanne would say.

Luanne believed in rules, but as long as it wasn't in her face, she usually let stuff go. I thought about my swim today. The official rules stated that no one could swim on the lake except in designated swim areas, unless you fell out of your boat. I always came back from a paddle with wet hair, and Luanne had been on the docks to meet me more than once.

"Fell out again?" She would grin.

"Yes, I'm very clumsy out there." I would smile back.

Thinking of Luanne reminded me of our plan. A glance at my phone told me I was late, but it didn't matter. I threw on a T-shirt and some long pants, grabbed my bottle and a glass, and headed up to Lu's cabin.

CHAPTER 4

LUANNE'S CABIN WAS PERCHED ON the gravel road that led to the pavilion. It was a newer building, but it tried to mimic the look of the original cabins. In front of her place there usually sat three or four lounge chairs, depending on her mood. They were aluminum framed and bore red cushions that had faded to pink. She liked to brag about having picked them up for ten dollars at a country garage sale. They'd gotten at least a thousand bucks' worth of sitting time over the years. If she didn't want company, all of the chairs but hers would be leaned against the cabin. You were not to sit uninvited. This was Luanne's summer living room, and she wasn't fond of unwelcome guests.

"Si'down!" she yelled to me from inside after I shouted a "hello."

The sun found a new favorite place for the day. Amber lights glowed from a few of the cabins. Once sitting, I pulled the serenity deep into my lungs and exhaled some stress with a long sigh. Lu was running around inside with the phone tucked between her shoulder and her head so her hands would be free. She was yelling at one of her kids while dishes clattered.

"I didn't tell you to keep the change. That was my money. I gave it to you to buy yourself lunch this week, not a concert ticket."

I was afraid for the person on the other side.

"I don't give a rat's ass if you ate free dirt all week. It's my money! You stole my money to buy that ticket, and trust me, you're gonna pay me back…this conversation is over. Tell your sisters I love them. Goodbye. I love you too, but you're gonna have to work that money off." She came out of the cabin with the phone in her hand and a glass in the other.

"Can you believe these kids? So spoiled," she said.

"Mine are too, although I fear it's my own fault."

"I started working as soon as I wanted anything that wasn't absolutely necessary. My parents didn't give me nothin'. These kids love to eat out, they want new clothes constantly, and then they have the balls to take my money. They think they are entitled to everything I got!"

"Amen," I said. My own fear of dying before the boys were grown had made me somewhat guilty of spoiling them. I was starting to see the repercussion in my oldest son, Jack Jr. I'd recently heard him making fun of a kid for having an outdated phone. He'd had his own iPhone taken away for the weekend for that comment, but I'd really wanted to toss it in the garbage. He had the teenage disease, and it scared me.

We sat in the dusk while the birds sang parting lullabies and the chirping bugs took over the choir. There was no need for a flashlight, but the sun had done all it could do for the day. I could see the shadow of a figure coming up the road.

"Here comes Maddy!" Luanne said.

Maddy was a special education teacher who also wrote grants for waterfront clean up in Brooklyn. She was getting ready for her daughter's wedding and had organized a community garden for inner-city kids. I found her to be beautiful, but not in a conventional way. She had big, dark, truthful eyes and curly black-and-silver hair that most women would have colored, but she "didn't have time for that shit." She still looked good in a swimsuit, even with that menopausal thickness we all had coming. She was robust and soft at the same time, like Mother Earth herself. Because she laughed easily and honestly, I'd fallen for her on our first meeting. If you didn't like Maddy, you were the problem, not her.

I didn't wait for Maddy to reach us; I walked to meet her with excitement. We hugged and strolled back to Luanne's while chatting and catching up.

"Where's Henry?" I asked. Henry was Maddy's husband, a grizzly bear of a man with a generous heart.

"In the cabin, playing the guitar. The other woman, I call her," she chuckled.

"Sidown," Luanne told her. The two of them had raised their children together in camp and were great friends. They both lived in the city and saw each other regularly there too. Maddy was one of the very few people who didn't piss Luanne off. I considered myself lucky that I was also in that small group. I loved these women, especially when they were together. They had a wonderful relationship that had transcended friendship. Over the years, they had given each other advice about the kids, mourned the loss of parents, and talked each other through dilemmas. They were soul sisters to each other and had generously allowed me in.

The three of us caught up with each other's lives the way women do. We talked about our kids and our current projects. I gave them the light version of what was going on with me and Jack.

"I just need some time to myself," I said. They nodded in support.

We fell into tales about our kids' antics that devolved into the kind of laughter that was always present when we were together. Luanne had the best stories, and Maddy and I listened with full attention.

"So she's sitting on the sofa, and I'm yelling at her for something she hadn't done that day, and she turns and mumbles something to the back of the sofa like a freakin' lunatic. I thought she was losing her mind! I say 'Whadaya crazy?' and she says, 'I'm talking to Voldemort.' And I say, 'You're talking to Voldemort?'—thinking she had gone freakin' nuts—'What's he sayin'?' and she says, 'He told me to tell you to shut up.'"

Maddy was laughing hysterically. I was holding my breath waiting for the tale to end with her wrath.

"'Voldemort told me to shut up?'" Luanne repeated, like an angry man in a bar about to duke it out. "I asked, just to make sure I had it freakin' straight. And she nodded her head yes. So I say, 'You tell him that I am going to kick his ass, and then I am going to kick *your* ass!'"

Now we were both dying, laughing into the darkness with an echo that was probably carried across the lake.

"So she whispers something to the sofa back, and then she turns around and says, 'Voldemort told me to tell you he's sorry.'"

"You need to write these down, Lu," I told her when I could contain myself again.

We sat in silence for a few moments—old enough friends to not need the words—until the dark silhouette of a thin figure came toward us from the road. When she got closer, I recognized her as the woman I'd met during my earlier swim. She was wearing a cotton turtleneck shirt with thick red sweatpants—the kind with elastic around the ankles. A long robe seemed to be serving as an overcoat. Tube socks sagged around her needle-like legs and took the shape of her big toe as they were forced into flip-flops. Her wild gray hair was restrained only by an elastic-banded headlamp, making her look like a walking light post. I was sweating just looking at her.

"Oh shit," I said as I wiped the tears off my face.

"So you've met Emily English, our new member?" Maddy asked in a whispered.

"Oh God, this woman is such a pain in my ass," Luanne added in a not-so-low voice.

We were silent as the woman made her way to us.

"Hi, Emily," Maddy finally said, always the kind one.

"I can hear your racket from my cabin," she stated, looking at the wine bottle and then back at us. "My screen door isn't closing properly. The mosquitoes are eating me alive."

"Keep your door shut and open your windows instead. Those screens are fine," Luanne said with little patience.

"I like to have my door open and get a good cross breeze, especially on a night like this. It's hot. Mosquitoes are a health hazard. I could get West Nile." Then she looked down at me and asked, "Who are you?" No smile. No hello.

Her headlamp shone so brightly that I had to put my hand over my eyes.

"I'm Lee Harding. We met on the lake today," I said, trying to be nice.

"I know that. I just wanted to know your name," she said. "She was swimming off of the rock," she added, addressing Luanne now.

"That's none of your business, Emily," Luanne replied calmly. Her accent made it sound like "nunaya."

Emily looked appalled. "I just wanted you to know. I mean, it's a safety hazard, and the camp could be liable," she said indignantly.

"Lee fell out of her boat. What do you want me to do?" It wasn't really a question, but Emily stood there silently, her bright light making us all squint. "I'll talk to Bobby about your screen door tomorrow," Lu finally conceded. It was enough to make Emily happy, and she wandered off toward the restrooms across the road.

"She's gonna be the death of me. Or I am going to be the death of her. Whatever comes first," Luanne groaned.

"She's gonna be the death of somebody if they run into her in camp dressed like that," Maddy added.

"Lookin' like somethin' the kids tell stories about around the fire," chimed in Luanne.

Maddy and I were laughing hard again.

"They kicked her out of Johnson, you know," Maddy said, wiping tears from her eyes.

"She mentioned that she used to go there. Did they really kick her out?" I asked.

"Put it this way: every cabin was full on any dates she wanted," Luanne said.

As dusk settled into darkness, a loud crackling sound came from across the lake.

"GOOD EVENING, LADIES. A QUOTE FROM LEVITICUS," a high-pitched female voice proceeded to read a verse that had something to do with atonement. It seemed to be coming from across the lake.

"Speak of the devil," Maddy said.

"What the fuck is that?" I asked.

"It's coming from Johnson Camp. The church ladies brought their own sound system. Tom says he's asked them not to use it, but no luck."

"What? Why doesn't he tell them to hand it over or leave?" I asked.

"He needs the money." Luanne shrugged in her "What are you going to do?" kind of way.

"You have got to be kidding me," I said.

The screeching started again—a mix of static and bossiness. "LADIES, THIS IS YOUR FIVE-MINUTE WARNING FOR

CAMPFIRE. ALL CAMPERS MUST BE PRESENT FOR EVE-NING CAMPFIRE PRAYERS. IF YOU HAVE SOMETHING TO SHARE, OR A SPECIAL PRAYER REQUEST, PLEASE RUN IT BY YOUR GROUP LEADER FIRST."

"I am going to paddle over there and drown her," I said.

Maddy laughed. Luanne just shook her head.

"You think that's bad? She's gonna sing to you again at 6:45 a.m."

CHAPTER 5

SOMETIMES WHEN I'M ALONE I feel intensely free—as if I can endlessly push open the walls around me. That evening the cabin felt stuffy and small, however, and I was left alone with thoughts of a crumbling family.

I put some water in my bong and opened my little mason jar full of weed. The experience of smoking was ritualistic and slow with no concern of being caught. After three deep hits, I decided the heat was too much and what I needed was to go skinny-dipping. I took my clothes off and slipped on a black gauze beach cover. The simple act made my skin moist, and I fanned myself with an unread *New Yorker* before leaving the cabin.

The lower path to the swim dock would allow me to bypass Luanne's cabin. She would not approve of my destination. The docks were made up of a ramp that led from the shore to the large landing, a roped-off Olympic-sized swimming area, and a floating dock in the far center. The space between the large landing and the shore was deep and clear enough that you could see to the bottom on a good day.

As I headed down to the dock, I stood silently for a moment, thinking I heard voices. *Who else would be down here at this hour?* I was not interested in socializing, so I carefully stepped over roots and rocks as quietly as possible.

In between my place and the swim dock were three cabins; the closest to mine was Moe and Roz Martin's. They were old-timers. Moe had been coming since he was a child, Roz since she met Moe. She had sewn the curtains in all of the cabins—little ruffled forest scenes on a tension bar. On any busy weekend you'd find her doing a craft project at a picnic table for the kids in camp. I had acorn and twig Christmas ornaments that my boys had made at her table. There was a light on in the kitchen. If my lake friends were forest animals, Roz and Moe would be beavers, always up before dawn and working late into the night. I could hear the low hum of a radio as I walked past.

Therese Azzario's cabin was down the path from theirs. I noticed the glow of light from her kitchen window. She was the early bird, fluttering over the lake with her sails, always circling the water. Therese would be eating her breakfast on the dock first thing in the morning and then dragging her Sunfish out before the rest of us had our coffee.

The last cabin was Randy Foster and Delia Lopez's. I could see lights but heard nothing. I wondered if they were up by themselves or if Randy's teenage son was with them. They were the squirrel family, working and playing and chasing each other up trees.

An unseen branch whipped my face, and I whispered swear words and felt to see if there would be a mark. I took the steep path down to the docks, each irregular stair familiar in depth. My eyes adjusted to the dark. Where the lake opened to the sky I could make out the shapes of trees along the water's edge before the darkness of the forest. There were so many stars that I gasped at my own insignificance.

I was pretty high. I'd gotten some new weed from my Realtor. Since it was still illegal in New Jersey, I had to take what I could get. This time it was a strain called Blue Dream. I was calmly euphoric and yet felt a cerebral invigoration.

I stood at the water's edge and pulled my dress off, revealing my naked body to the watching celestials. My hair was feral with humidity and sticking to the back of my neck with sweat. I was barely liberated from my dress before the humid air started its attack and forced me to jump in.

The water was cold silk around my shoulders and breasts, cleansing me of the heat of the day, the sadness that had brought me here alone, the family memories, all crumbling around me like a sand sculpture, beautiful but impermanent. I wondered if it had ever been real. Another plunge, and the thoughts were rinsed away.

By the time I swam out to the swim dock, I had decided that it wasn't where I wanted to be and turned away, on my back this time, so I could stare into infinity. I was part of the lake now instead of just a visitor. I belonged to it. I touched my outer thighs, silken and fluid, and brought my hands to my full, buoyant breasts. On land I could only feel the ripples and sags of age approaching me, but there in the lake I was young again, weightless and firm and unrestrained. My legs kicked open, and the cold water touched my body, aggressively at first, then quietly as it warmed to my heat.

Self-conscious, I looked to the dock and thought I saw a figure standing by the trees. I reversed and swam silently back out, and when I turned around to look again, whoever it was had gone.

I don't know how long I stayed that night, but the air was cool against my damp skin when I returned to my cabin. My bed called for me like a hungry lover. It was pitch dark in the forest—miles and miles from the light pollution of New York City. Outside, a noisy symphony of wildlife amplified throughout camp: the string section of crickets, the bass sung by frogs on the shore, and the wind instruments of the cicadas. They played well that night, and I slept better than I had in weeks.

CHAPTER 6

I DREAMT I WAS IN prison, a guard shouting orders for me to get up. I opened my eyes and lifted my face from the mattress. My sheet had slipped off in the night, and my face was pressed against the bare mattress.

"EARLY BIRD CATCHES THE WORM, LADIES," a shrill voice chanted. "RISE AND SHINE FOR BREAKFAST AT EIGHT," and then proceeded to read a long Bible verse that had something to do with sin and godliness.

"Motherfucker!" I groaned.

I stumbled out of bed and looked into the tiny, warped mirror that was stuck on the wall in the bedroom while the voice from Johnson Camp repeated herself in entirety. There was a red circle on my cheek where I'd stuck to the mattress. My long dirty blonde hair was thick with matted lumps. As I started to comb them, the amplified voice made me angry and I pulled too hard. Sometimes I thought I was pretty, but lately the lines around my face screamed my age. I was almost forty and feeling it. No more dancing on tabletops. My youth was behind me. I swore again at the woman across the lake as if it were all her fault.

I made coffee in slow motion, grabbed a loaf of bread, and headed back over to the swim docks. There was a dear old friend that I liked to catch early morning. I hoped the demon of Johnson's Camp hadn't scared him off.

I began crumbling bread into the water, and dozens of sunfish raced toward the dusty fragments. When the food was gone, they waited on me to throw more, like a pack of swimming puppies. If I walked down the ramp, they'd follow me. I'd always been amazed that the little dummies were smart enough to follow me around. I felt bad that I was setting them up.

After a few moments, I got what I was waiting for. An enormous snapping turtle emerged rapidly and grabbed one of the little fishes whole. He made such a splash that a ripple moved across the pool. I jumped in surprise. He was mythologically large, taking my breath away each time I was lucky enough to see him.

"Hello, Stan!" I said to the shy hunter before he disappeared back to his home under the landing. "You're welcome."

The fish were back to their begging within seconds, apparently not missing their fallen comrade.

Stan had lived under the dock for as long as anyone remembered. There were people here who had been coming to camp for fifty years and swore they had known him all that time. No one could remember who had named him.

Snapping turtles are cranky when outside of the water. They have long necks that can reach all the way back to their legs. We all knew to stay away from Stan on those rare moments when he basked in the sun. In the water, though, he was shy and elusive. I used to worry that he'd bite my toes off, but he avoided people at all cost.

I looked across the lake toward Johnson Beach, where I could see women congregating under the demand of their leader. That woman had violated my sanctuary, and I was feeling the need for justice.

"Seriously, Luanne. I can't believe you haven't shut that woman up," I said when she joined me on the deck of the pavilion to drink coffee in one of the big chairs.

"I've tried everything. I called the Parks department. I called Tom. No one's done a thing."

"I'm going to kill her," I promised.

"Get in line."

A petite blonde woman in a faded red, tank-style swimsuit walked by without glancing in our direction. I admired her confidence; I always wore a dress over my suit in public, even when paddling. I had a pretty good figure, and I'm five foot ten, so I could get away with the few extra pounds I'd put on over the years, but for me, the thighs and butt needed to be covered. She was talking to a young man who looked our way and gave an awkward wave when he saw us looking at them.

I waved back.

"Hi, Therese!" I said in a voice that required a return salutation.

"Hi, Lee," she replied without turning around.

I looked at Luanne.

"It's not you, honey. It's all of us." She chuckled as I shook my head.

"Why do some of the old-timers think they own the camp?" I asked her, knowing full well she didn't have the answer.

"God likes them better than you," she joked flatly.

Even after eight summers at the lake, Therese still considered me a newbie. She'd grown up in this camp and felt a strong ownership of the place. She was also bound to it by tragedy—her twin brother had died here in the early sixties. He and his friends had been rough-housing, and someone had pushed him off of the dock. The lakeshore was full of large rocks, and he'd hit his head and drowned. It was a cautionary tale we all told our kids to keep them from impulsive be-havior by the water.

I often wondered if Therese would be a different person had her childhood not been scarred by tragedy. Death changes our perspec-tive. Maybe she would be softer and sillier. Or maybe she'd always been aloof. Once in a while I was able to break through and have a real conversation with her, but it was always me saying hello first, even if we were the only two people in the swim area.

Her petite body was loose and leathery, but she still had the fit shape of a lifelong paddler and swimmer, and her single process blonde head would have been more appropriate on a twenty-year-old girl. Luanne and Maddy called her Peter Pan. I admired her refusal to grow up but wondered if she was stunted somehow by her brother's death. Maybe he was her lost boy.

Therese was in charge of the swim docks and the lifeguards who worked on them. I figured she was training the boy she was with.

"Who's that?" I asked Luanne.

"You don't recognize him? That's Randy's son, Jacob."

"Jeez. He sure sprouted up. He's a lot cuter than his father."

Randy Foster was an odd-looking guy. He was short and muscu-lar and could have been attractive except that you could see the blood vessels under his skin. It wasn't his fault that his veins were so close to his skin. It was his fault, however, that he never stopped talking about himself. He could have been attractive.

"You got that right," Luanne said, shaking her head.

Jacob had made the transition from boy to man, physically any-way. He had the tight chest and the narrow waist of youth, lean and tall. His sandy blond hair was thick and messy. He looked like a Ralph Lauren model in his red swimsuit.

"Randy's been plopping his ass down in my chair for the last week," Luanne complained. "Once he's there, I can't get him out.

Finally, I just told him not to sit there unless I offered, like everyone else. The guy is clueless."

"He's doesn't speak body language," I added, thinking about how hard it was to get away from him once he started talking. Randy liked to talk about himself, and I liked to avoid him. He was a dingbat. I'd known him for eight years, and although I could tell you his life story, he didn't know a thing about me. He only exported data.

"He's clueless," she said, shaking her head the way she so often did at those many people who annoyed her.

"Who else is in camp?" I asked.

She thought a moment. "Roz and Moe. And Marge and Lester." Marge and Lester Rice were sixty-something siblings. They were private people. I hadn't seen either one since my arrival, even though their cabin was just behind mine. They considered themselves lords of the camp; Marge behaved like it anyway. I'd met her dozens of times over the years, but I'd bet she still didn't know my name. Their parents had been the first to occupy the Rice cabin, as we called it, back when the camp was handed over to the club. They had survived coup after coup in camp leadership since.

Marge served on the board of directors of the club and ruled like she was Queen Elizabeth. In fact, she'd been in office almost as long, from what Luanne had told me. Her brother Lester was grumpy and rigid. He looked older than Marge, but she treated him like a child, ordering him about. He was usually found trailing her. I'd once seen him carry a milk jug of urine to the bathrooms. It was all I could think about when I looked at him after that.

"Weird that there aren't any other kids here this week," I said.

"It's only Tuesday. They'll be here on Friday," she warned. "Don't rush it. My peace and quiet will be over."

The weekdays were so lovely in camp. By Friday, day users arrived from the city and surrounding suburbs, and cars lined the road all the way out to the gate. Luanne spent her weekends walking up and down the road, collecting day fees, telling people to move, and directing them to the right campsites. On top of that, her husband and at least one daughter would be here too, placing their own demands on her. You got your best Luanne on the weekdays.

She ran off to do one of her many jobs, and I headed back to my cabin. I thought about phoning Jack but let the idea slip away.

As I approached my cabin, I saw Emily coming toward me. My body tensed at the sight of her. She was wearing a wide-brimmed paddler's hat that randomly rose and fell around her head and a faded Hawaiian shirt so thin I could see the frail outline of her bony shoulder blades. Her pants were tucked into her socks again. A fanny pack was stuffed to the point near explosion.

"Good morning, Lee," she said like we were old friends.

"Good morning, Emily." I kept walking to let her know that I had somewhere to be, but she stepped in front of me and began to talk.

"Can you believe that Bobby? He still hasn't fixed my screen door."

"Well, I'm sure he'll get to it," I said. "How are you feeling this morning?"

I could see she was revving up to tell me a long story about her aches and pains, but Roz Martin walked up the path and greeted us before she could get going. Roz was a short and thick little grandmother type, but she was playful and active in a youthful way. You got the idea that she could still build her own house if she wanted to. She was wearing a simple cotton V-neck T-shirt and shorts with sneakers—her practical uniform at the lake.

"Did you take a morning paddle?" Roz asked me after inquiring about my family.

"No. I woke up cranky this morning. I was planning on sleeping in, but that screaming evangelist across the lake shocked me out of bed."

They both looked puzzled.

"You didn't hear that woman from Johnson this morning?"

"Oh! Yes," Roz laughed. "She's a real treat isn't she? I think I may be getting used to it."

"Well, I called the Parks Service to complain when I was in town yesterday. They told me they were looking into it," Emily said. Her overblown sense of justice compelled her to believe it would happen.

"Summer is going to be over before they do anything about it," Roz said.

"I'm going to paddle over and steal the damned sound system myself," I stated.

They both looked at me like I was nuts.

"I'm serious."

"Well, you could get arrested for that." Emily seemed appalled at the idea of breaking the law. She stared at me, waiting for an answer with eyes wide open.

"Only if I get caught." I smiled. "You'll keep my secret, right, Emily?"

"Oh, I know lots of secrets around here," she said with a creepy smile.

"What kinds of secrets do people around here keep?" I asked, my head tilted while I waited for her answer.

"They wouldn't be secrets if I told you what they were, now would they?" she said, looking to Roz as she spoke. I reminded myself that this woman was a bit of a loon, and I didn't dig deeper.

Roz didn't seem to respond to her comment at all, and I wondered if I had imagined that it was directed toward her. "Well, it's been nice seeing you ladies. I have a date with my boat now," I said, shaking my head. Emily's personality had the same effect as bug repellent. I needed to fly away.

I stopped at my cabin to grab a few things and headed down the trail toward the dock. When I got there, Marge and Lester Rice were there, gearing up for a paddle in a Grumman canoe. Marge had lobsters on her pink shorts and looked like she should be in Nantucket. Lester was pressed and neat like Marge had dressed him, in a royal blue polo and white shorts with perfect creases down the legs.

"Hello, Lee. I was wondering when we were going to see you this summer," Marge said with a warm smile.

It was always strange for me to talk to Marge because I knew that she could be a real viper. She had an artful way of digging at someone through what she portrayed as compliments. "Hi, Marge, hello, Lester. I can't believe it's taken me this long to get up here. We've had a really busy summer. Jack Jr. played on a traveling soccer league, which took a bunch of our weekends," I explained. "But I am here now, and I may never go home," I said.

Little did she know, I meant it. I was planning on staying at least as long as the boys were in camp, which was a month. As long as I could keep a cabin, I would be here. Even if that meant staying in the bunk house with Freddie.

"Where are you two headed?" I asked.

She held up a thermos. "Blueberry Island. Did you get any yet? The berries are spectacular this year. So sweet."

I held up my jar and smiled. "That's my mission also."

Lester was already in the boat, staring straight ahead, waiting patiently while Marge continued to chat with me. She asked after my husband and boys like everyone there did. I gave my twenty-second camp speech on where they were and pretended that life was perfect because Marge didn't want to know the truth. I mean, who did really? But Marge had no interest.

"You mean that Jack isn't coming at all? How brave of you to come by yourself," she said. "Lester dear, remember to stabilize," she said. He placed the wooden paddle across the boat and the dock, so it couldn't rock from sided to side. Marge did the same as she stepped in and had a perfect landing in the front of the canoe.

As they paddled away in the old aluminum boat, I thought of how it was all wrong for them. They should have been in one of the old wooden classics that hung from the rafters of the pavilion collecting dust. They were relics, like an old postcard in faded pastel.

CHAPTER 7

RED GLIDED THROUGH THE WATER slowly, so I could get close enough to pick the wild blueberries from the branches that hung over the lake. The jar I had tucked between my legs was almost full. I loved being here in late spring when the mountain laurel that lined the lake dropped their confetti of pink blossoms onto the surface as a celebration of summer's arrival. But July was a great time to enjoy the fruits of the season with my breakfasts and in my bourbons. There is nothing better than a blueberry-and-basil Old Fashioned.

In the shallows, fallen logs rested in preservation, the water perfect and clear around them. The lakeshore was rocky, and at almost any point I could get out and stand on a granite slab if stranded. I guided Red around the peninsula that Camp Montego clung to, rowing by the swim area. Therese was sitting under a large green umbrella that protected the lifeguards from the daily beating of sunshine. Jacob had swum out to one of the floating docks to scrub goose droppings off of the deck. I pulled up along side him as he worked.

"And people think lifeguarding is glamorous," I joked. I got a smile out of him, which was pretty good considering he was a cranky teenager.

"Are Jack Jr. and Max coming up?" he asked, continuing to sweep.

I was surprised he had asked. My youngest had always felt bullied by the boy, so his older brother Jack felt the need to protect him. They had never involved parents in their squabbles, but I knew that my boys didn't care much for Jacob.

"No. They're away at camp for the month. I guess it's pretty dead around here without other kids, right?"

"It's pretty boring," he said in monotone. "Therese lets me take the Sunfish out sometimes. And Roz and Moe are here at least." He pushed the brush while he talked, never really looking at me, and then added, "The weekend should be busy."

I pushed off in the direction of Johnson Beach, in hopes of convincing Tom Johnson to stop the noise pollution his camp was producing. The water was glassy calm, and the afternoon sun beat on my back as I paddled across the lake. I'd made the trip many times over the years with my family. The memory of the kids splashing and falling out of their boats on purpose and the sounds of laughter on a summer day echoing across the lake filled my mind. Jack and I would look at each other in those simple moments—a look that transcended language—pride and gratitude and love, all amplified. A sense of mourning weighed heavily on my heart.

Johnson Beach was crowded with women of all shapes and sizes. Plastic water bottles and chip bags were strewn about with abandon. I pulled a soda can out of the water as I paddled near and dropped it into the garbage barrel in the sand. Clusters of ladies were sitting in the shade by the lakeside. A short round woman rose to approach me. She was wearing a terrycloth beach cover and a large sunhat. Enormous sunglasses hid most of her fat little face.

"Excuse me, but the camp is closed for a private event," she said, her high voice instantly recognizable as the reason for my visit.

She couldn't have been five feet tall, but she was a fierce little thing. She had no problem shooing me off the beach.

"I'm aware of that," I said, not feeling very friendly. "Is Tom around?"

"He isn't here, dear. He went into town for some supplies."

"Oh shit. Okay."

The little fat woman's mouth closed into a tight "Oooh!" and her eyes went wide with indignation. Her clan of ladies watched me like I wore the scarlet letter.

"I came to complain about the noise. Do you know anything about that? We can hear it nonstop across the lake, and it's a real intrusion on our time here. I believe it's also a violation of park rules."

The whole clan stared silently. I got back in my boat before they strapped me to the empty lifeguard stand and lit it—and me—on fire.

My cove felt tainted after yesterday's run-in with Emily, so I paddled back to camp cranky, my head filled with the disappointment that expectations often bring. Once Red was secured, I returned to my cabin and took a few hits off of my bong. *Wouldn't the church ladies love to see me now?* The room filled with a thick, sweet, skunky smell. The frustrations of the morning fell away as the high took the edge off and made everything and everyone beautiful again. I grabbed a beach towel and headed to the swim docks.

I walked past the gravel parking lot. At the top of the hill I noticed Emily heading to the bathrooms with cleaning supplies. Emily was wearing gloves up to her elbows, and her wild hair was tucked away in a bandana that was wrapped around her head. She reminded me of the cleaning woman character from the *Carol Burnett Show* as she struggled with a bucket and mop and checked her pockets as if she'd forgotten something critical.

Everyone took turns doing chores around camp. Apparently it was Emily's week for bathroom duty. The building that housed the restrooms was a simple A-frame structure divided down the center by a six-foot wall (meaning that the top was open and you could hear everything from each side). There were several toilet stalls and a shower on each side. A colony of trapped moths usually fluttered about, and the place was a daddy longlegs sanctuary. I always checked my hair for spiders when leaving the stalls.

Jack and I mailed checks to pay for things like cabin repairs and new play equipment for the kids. We weren't here often enough to be on the schedule, and we weren't planning to enter the lottery for a cabin, which was how campers were able to get a five-year lease. The more work you did around camp, the better chance you had of being entered to win. No one signed up for bathroom duty unless they wanted credit for the cabin lottery. I wondered whose leases were up. After five years (or more when they won consecutively, as many had), the cabins began to feel like home.

Luanne was knitting in front of her place. All of the chairs except for the one she was sitting in were put away. This meant, "Leave me alone."

"Hey, Lu," I said, walking past her.

"Hey," she said, looking up from her knitting. "Whaduhyah up to?"

"Just went to see Tom about that little demon who woke me up this morning. He wasn't there, but she was."

"You met her?" Luanne was on full alert.

"Yeah. I'll tell you about it later. The lake is calling me for a swim." I walked off through the pavilion and down the steep steps to the swim area.

I dropped my towel and jumped in like a little kid whose time out was over. Unlike last night, a day swim allowed me to be eye level with the trees on the shore. The perspective made the sky appear peri-winkle and the clouds surreal. I loved to spin in circles to catch every angle of the soft mountaintops around me. The pavilion rose from the top of the hill through the trees like it had grown up with them.

The calm I got from weed slowed me down enough to enjoy the enhanced beauty of the surroundings. I was present in a way that I hadn't figured out how to be without its help. Therese sat silently under a large umbrella, consumed by a magazine. Jacob did his job, keeping his eye on me as I bobbed around. I kicked my limbs freely and moved without restraint until I finally ended up at one of the floating docks and climbed up on the deck to bask in the sun. My mind returned to how euphoric last night's swim had been.

Across the lake, Johnson Beach was empty. The little loud mouth had announced that it was lunchtime a few moments earlier. The boards of the dock were hot against my wet back. I watched a cloud move slowly across the sky and began to drift off. A few moments later the dock tilted slightly, alerting me to someone holding onto the ladder.

"Sorry to wake you," said a familiar voice from the water.

"Hi, Moe!" Moe Martin was one of my favorite lake people. He was that uncle that everybody wished they had, full of coin tricks and silly jokes. My boys adored him. A retired accountant, he and his wife and two kids, now grown, had spent all of their summers at the lake.

Moe was round and soft in every way. His hair had parted ways with his head long ago. He wasn't wearing his glasses and had that squinty look that those with bad eyesight often give you when they are trying to bring you into focus. He reminded me of Mr. Magoo.

"Where are the boys?" He didn't climb the ladder, but instead addressed me as he moved to keep himself afloat.

I knew it would be his first question. "They're away at camp. Jack is tied up at work. I figured I would spend a week or two with my lake friends."

"Make sure you send those boys to college close to home. You don't want to be up here without them forever," he said as he did every year. Poor Moe and Roz! They'd raised a family with the intention of celebrating life with them later, only to find their kids had different dreams. Both of their children had gone west for college, never to return. Camp was a little too rustic for their upper-middleclass offspring, who preferred beach resorts to camp dirt. Moe and Roz would be the last generation of a long line of Martin campers at Montego.

"I won't forget those words, Moe." I hoped my boys wouldn't abandon me like that, but I would never actually say so to them. They had to choose their own path.

The truth was that Jack and I had discussed moving back west ourselves in the next few years. The thought of leaving this summer paradise made me sad. Would we return to the East Coast just to stay at the lake? I doubted it. And I doubted it would be the same if we did. It seemed that my destiny was to be torn between two coasts for the rest of my life.

"What are you doing for dinner tonight, honey? Want to come by our place? I don't know what Roz is whipping up, but I know she'd be happy to have you."

"Yes!" I replied. "What can I bring?"

"Just bring yourself, hon. You know how she is. We'll have enough food to feed an army."

I laughed, knowing it was true, but still reminded myself to pick up some dessert when I went into town.

CHAPTER 8

HARRISBURG WAS FIVE MILES DOWN the park road. It was where we bought ice and beer and snacks while we were in camp. It was a depressed little country town, left abandoned when the freeway bypassed it decades ago. Once grand homes grew tall weeds in their front yards and displayed bed sheets as curtains. There was a general store, a dive bar, and a gas station, unremarkable basics with the exception of Earl's Road House. I'd often said Earl's was my favorite restaurant in the world, and it wasn't a lie. The place was exactly as a road house should be: a separate parking lot for Harleys, moose heads over the bar, and antique signs from long gone competitions sprawled randomly across the walls. Earl's was built along a creek, and the owner had had the brilliant idea to bring sand in and create a beach. A row of colorful Adirondack chairs faced the water. There was no better place to for a cold drink, which is what Maddy and I did before we had lunch on the deck.

"It's so tense at camp," she said. "Can you feel it?"

We were lying back in the sloping chairs, looking up at the trees that overhung the creek.

"Not really. What do you think is going on?" I asked.

"I just feel it in the air. Maybe it's the coming lottery," she said.

"How many cabins are up for lottery this year? Is yours?" I asked.

"No. Not ours. Nobody wants our out-of-the-way tent cabin anyway," Maddy said. "That's the beauty of it. They all want to fight for the core cabins with docks. We love it up on the hill with all the other tent cabins, which are often empty. There are three cabins at the end of their five-year leases this year," she told me. "And six applicants, including those three who already have the cabins now.

"So what's up with you? Something's going on. You aren't normally dreary."

I took a deep breath. "Jack and I are having big trouble." Just saying it made me choke up a little bit.

"I have no doubt that you guys will be fine," Maddy said with confidence.

"Everyone keeps saying that to me, but I really can't stand him these days, Maddy. I can't find forgiveness for the tiniest things he says."

"Lee, I've been married to Henry for twenty-five years. Do you know how many times I've felt like that about him? Welcome to marriage. Pretty soon Jack's face will be tolerable to you again, and before you know it, you'll be missing his touch."

"I don't know," I said doubtfully. "I feel like we've grown into two different people."

"Were you ever the same two people?"

I thought back. *Nope.* We sat quietly until they called us to our table. I could barely get up from the chair I was so relaxed.

"Someday I am just going to sit here all day, and no one will call me or make me go anywhere. I won't have to drive, and I won't get bossed around." I knew I sounded like a brat, but that was how it felt. I was a little annoyed that I had to watch myself because I had to drive. One or two bourbon and sodas was all I could do.

"We can come tomorrow. I'll drive, and you can sit here and get hammered," she offered, laughing. "Better yet, we can make Luanne drive. She's a great designated driver."

After lunch we went to the General Store for some groceries. Maddy and Henry had also been invited to dinner at Roz and Moe's. Knowing Roz, the whole camp was probably invited. We strolled through the tiny aisles that sold sample toothpaste, bug spray, and playing cards alongside bagged and boxed foods with no expiration dates. I bought "dessert," which was a factory-made box of chocolate chip cookies and some kind of coffee cake. It was all they had.

For the first time in days my phone had service. Jack had called five times and left two messages. I listened to make sure the kids were all right, but wasn't ready to call him back. I texted him instead: *I'm fine. Need some time to think.*

Maddy had wandered over to the wall of refrigerated items and wasn't moving. I reminded her of why we where there, and she laughed and thanked me. We headed back to the car and soon pulled into camp. With the exception of my tires on the gravel, it was dead quiet. It was nap time for Maddy and would soon be for me also.

I headed to my place, where I poured myself a bourbon and soda and sat on the back patio with a copy of Thoreau's *Walden*. It had been my mother's book, and each time I opened it, I looked at the bookplate: an inked owl with the words "Ex Libris" engraved on it along with her name. My mother died when I was ten years old. The bookplate was like touching a part of her.

My eldest sister, Lacy, had inherited our mother's china; my sister Alice had her wedding rings. I'd chosen a trunk full of leather-bound books. They'd been a gift from a wealthy aunt who'd sent my mother one each year for her birthday, Christmas, and landmark events. I'd read them all when I was younger but had recently begun to go through them again. When the trunk was open, I could smell the must of our house in San Francisco: the scent of old ink and optimism.

I went to the woods because I wished to live deliberately, to front only the essential facts of life, and see if I could learn what it had to teach, and not, when I came to die, discover that I had not lived, Thoreau wrote. I understood him completely today. Living in nature stripped everything else away, but not the "essential facts of life."

Unfortunately, these essentials were my family, and all of this quiet time allowed me to think of what breaking that unit apart would really mean. *Did I really want to make Jack move out of the house? Should I be the one to leave? Would that be abandoning the kids?* A blanket of sadness wrapped around me, and I looked for some distraction that would not mean tears. I turned again to *Walden*, but fell asleep before I could turn the page twice.

I dreamed I was in Haiti with Jack. Someone was shooting at us, and although he didn't say it, I knew it was my fault. The *tap tap tap* of the bullets kept coming. I awoke to the sound echoing through the woods. After a few startled seconds, I realized it was hammering, probably coming from Bobby's cabin.

Luanne showed up on my patio some time later. She plopped herself down—I did not have to invite her—and started in on Bobby. "I am ready to kill him. Really. He finally gets over to Emily's to fix the goddamned door so she'll shut up, and she's not there, so he doesn't do it. I took the fuckin' door off myself and brought it over to him. He's useless."

"Why wouldn't he take it off?" I asked her.

"'It's an invasion of her privacy,'" she mimicked. "I didn't even have to open it to get the screen door off. Just fix it!"

I was surprised Bobby and Luanne hadn't gotten into a fistfight yet. "Just sock him in the face next time, Lu," I said.

She looked at me with furrowed brows.

"I'm serious. Just punch his lights out. Kick him in the balls, and make him fall down. Then kick him in the stomach while he's down."

She tried to hold a straight face but couldn't. She let out a laugh.

"You can take him," I said.

"You know it," she replied with a wry smile.

"I have white wine," I offered. "And bourbon. And weed." I laughed.

"Naw. Later. Are you going to Roz and Moe's?"

"Yeah. What time are we supposed to be there?"

"Now," she said and waited for me to grab my dessert so we could walk over together.

Roz never did anything halfway. She'd lit her patio with little battery-powered tea lights and some hanging lanterns. Frank Sinatra was playing from inside. Her picnic table was covered with salads and platters of vegetables.

They'd remembered that I was a vegetarian. That meant a lot to me. I usually ended up eating lots of sides, but Moe had an enormous Portobello on the grill for me, separated from the rest of the burgers. Roz, Moe, Henry, and Luanne sat at the freshly painted picnic table, and Freddie, Maddy, and I gathered in chairs around the fire. For a while, the forest echoed with laughter as we listened to each other's tales from time away from the lake.

After dinner, Roz laid out ingredients for s'mores, including homemade peanut butter cookies instead of graham crackers. For a moment, I thought of calling out for my kids, who would have been all over the dessert, but then I remembered with a pang of sadness that they were far from me.

Freddie was on his second s'more, and I shook my head in admiration. "How do you stay so thin, Freddie?" I said. "If I ate the way you did, I would weigh two hundred pounds."

"You would still be beautiful, Lee. Those inquisitive green eyes of yours can't be stopped by some extra calories," he said. His fading Caribbean accent made everything sound just a little more sweet.

"Aw. Thanks, Freddie," I said.

"You just have to do twenty miles a day out on the lake," Maddy said. "It's no secret; the guy never stops moving."

"That's not true, Maddy. Last night I leaned back on my boat and watched the stars for at least an hour. I'm not always moving out there."

I pictured him on his boat in the middle of the cove, the vast sky above him in breathtaking splendor. "Wow." I sighed. "That must have been incredible."

Freddie nodded. "It was spectacular."

"Thanks so much for dinner, Roz. Everything was incredible as usual," Maddy said, rubbing her belly as she leaned back in her chair.

"Yes, thank you," the rest of us added.

"You're all welcome. This may be our last year in this place, so we're going to do a lot of dining and celebrating this summer."

"What are you talking about?" I asked. I looked around for surprised faces. Apparently I was the only one who didn't know.

"Our lease is up this year," Roz said sadly after a moment.

"It's hotter than Hades tonight. Who's up for a swim?" Moe chimed in, clapping his hands together.

"Nothing like a moonlight swim," Maddy said.

I had questions, but apparently no one wanted to talk about it so I let it go.

I decided to go back to my cabin and changed, somewhat grudgingly, into my still wet suit. I met the others down at the dock. Henry, Moe, Maddy, and I were the only ones who got in. Freddie went back to his cabin. I guessed he would be getting ready for his nightly paddle. Randy and Delia showed up for what was probably supposed to be a romantic swim only to find us all bobbing around off the dock.

Delia Lopez had a pretty face even without makeup. There was a sweetness about her—almost victim sweet. She had connected with Randy midlife, and rumor had it her first marriage was abusive. Luckily, Randy regarded her with the appropriate worship, as she was quite a beautiful woman, inside and out. Her long dark hair blanketed her shoulders in soft ringlets, and I felt a moment of envy. My own hair could not be convinced to do anything but play dead. She wore boxer shorts over her bikini, and I could see a slight six-pack from all of the running and yoga she did.

Randy stood next to her, wearing a tank top with his bathing suit. He was fit and toned without being too muscular. In the dark, you couldn't see his transparent skin. He stood an inch or two shorter than Delia. His head of thick cropped sandy blond hair and his strong square face could have been handsome if he were able to keep his mouth shut.

The water was refreshingly cold and cured the swelter of the humidity. The moon was a thin glowing crescent over the pavilion at the top of the hill.

"Breathtaking," Delia said, looking up.

Just as the silent moment filled us all with peace, a high-pitched command came from across the lake and announced prayer time in the dining hall, her voice breaking the quiet that defined night.

Several sighs and murmurs of complaints came from dark spots in the water where we had all scattered.

"That's it! I am confiscating that sound system. Who's coming with me?"

"Whaddaya, crazy? You'll get arrested."

"Only if I get caught," I said. I was feeling buzzed from the several drinks I'd had at dinner.

"I'm in!" Maddy announced. "You're coming too, Henry," she informed her husband.

"Me too," said Moe.

"Oh no you're not!" Roz said.

Moe looked disappointed, but not enough to rebel.

"I'll go," said Randy. I was very surprised by his bravery. "Let's take the war canoe."

Delia also joined us as we swam out to the enormous canoe, which was always anchored a few hundred feet off shore. The boat could hold fifteen paddlers and was used for regattas.

I could hear Luanne on the dock, pacing and shouting. "Honest to God I could lose my job, you guys. I didn't see nothing. I don't know anything about this."

"You weren't even here, Luanne. You were never here!" I whisper-shouted from the water. I couldn't help but laugh. She looked like a nervous dog watching its owner sail out in a storm.

We climbed clumsily into the massive canoe and paddled over to Johnson Beach, shushing each other as we made plans and giggled our way across the lake.

"Put the life jackets on!" I could hear Luanne say from the dock.

We all ignored her and paddled on into darkness with only the lights from Johnson Camp to guide us.

"Holy God," were the last words we heard from her as we cruised into the darkness.

We tried to unload silently when we got to shore, but Maddy fell out and landed in the water, laughing hysterically. We pulled her out and secured the boat on the beach before heading up the hill into camp. Maddy tripped again on the unlit stairs. I was snorting from trying not to laugh, but I couldn't contain myself. We stood quietly to hear if we'd been discovered before heading up the steep hill.

The dining hall lights were on, and we could see the women gathered there together, hands held and eyes closed in prayer.

"Try the kitchen first," I said, thinking the woman would have broadcast from where she was meeting.

"I'll go in," Henry announced bravely. He was a big man and not exactly quiet.

"Umm. It's a woman's retreat, Henry. Why don't you let one of us go in, so if we get caught, we can pretend to be strays?" I said.

"She's already seen you, Lee. I'll go," Maddy suggested.

"No offense, Maddy, but I am the sober one. I'll go," said Delia.

She was right. Neither Maddy nor I were in any shape to tiptoe. Delia slipped into the kitchen and came back out quickly holding a box and a megaphone and some loose cords. We squealed with excitement and headed back down the hill.

As soon as we hit the beach, there was trouble—Tom Johnson was standing over the war canoe waiting for us. "What are you doing here?" he demanded.

We all just stood there, Delia behind us. We gathered instinctually to hide her.

"We were looking for you, Tom. We were going to ask you to shut that woman up," I said. "I came by today, but you weren't here. That mean little friend of yours shooed me off the beach."

He looked kind of rattled. I wondered what he was doing down here and saw that he too had been on the water tonight. His shorts were wet, but not his T-shirt. Tom Johnson was a big man; I guessed he was in his late forties. His father had had heart problems, and Tom had had to skip college to keep the camp up and help his mother out. He was married to a local girl, and they had two small children. Whether he had liked it or not, his life was the camp.

"She is no friend of mine. I promise you that. I'm sorry about the noise, folks, but business is business." He was letting them do whatever they wanted. Times must have been really tough.

We backed our way to the boat, and I saw Randy covering for Delia while she quietly placed the equipment inside the war canoe.

"Well, it was a nice night for a paddle anyway," I said as I got in the vessel.

"They won't be here next summer," he said apologetically as we paddled off.

"Oh my God! We are so busted!" Maddy whispered.

"We're in big trouble," Henry agreed.

"That was just weird. He was acting very strange," I said.

"Yeah, he seemed more nervous about seeing us than we were about getting caught there," Delia added.

We were joyous and relieved on our paddle back. I sat in back of the boat, my paddle our rudder. My eyes had adjusted wonderfully to the night, exposing the silhouette of the mountains around us, black and jagged from the tree lines. With a sweet and perfect pitch, Delia began singing a song about the moon that I had never heard before. We paddled on, the magic of adventure and nature silencing us. The view of Montego Camp from the water was a wonderful sight in the darkness and reminded me of a fairytale. The porch lights from the cabins glowed like beacons on the forested hillside.

We agreed to leave the sound system in the war canoe. Getting it out without another boat to carry it in would mean ruining it, and we planned on bringing it back eventually. Luanne was waiting for us at the dock when we got back. Roz and Moe had gone to bed. She was pacing back and forth, her skinny little body tight with nervous energy. As we pulled our wet bodies up the ladder at the dock, we all faced Luanne with fear.

"We got caught," I confessed.

"Oh God! Oh shit! What happened?" I thought she was going to hyperventilate. Luanne loved rules, and we had broken them. She was visibly shaken, more than I'd expected. If I'd known she was going to be this upset, I wouldn't have gone.

"Tom was on the beach when we were leaving. He didn't see the sound system, but he knows we were there. We told him we came to complain about the noise."

"He was acting really weird," said Randy, who had only stopped talking about it during Delia's song. I wondered if she'd started singing just to shut him up.

"Yeah, well, I'm going bed. I hope you guys didn't get me fired."

I was feeling a little guilty on my way back to the cabin. What would my boys think if they knew? Jack would have flipped out. Between the alcohol and the exhaustion, I didn't care what Jack thought.

CHAPTER 9

WHEN I OPENED MY EYES the next morning, the forest sat in the quiet that accompanied sunrise. My head was pounding from the abuse of alcohol. Facing my bed I could see an enormous spider—Halloween decoration sized—on the window screen. I crawled out of bed and crept closer to see if she was inside or out. If I frightened her, she hid it well and stood her ground. Maybe she thought I wouldn't see her if she stayed perfectly still.

She was outside the screen, which gave me great relief. Now brave, I looked closer at her gracefully striped legs. Her wondrous body was compartmentalized, each piece its own work of art in rust and black. Outside was silence, the frogs and insects and birds all sleeping. We, the giant and the tiny creature that so often sent me screaming, were alone in the dawn.

I poured myself a large glass of water and went back to bed, keeping one throbbing eye on the spider as if she might've brought tools to attempt a break in. At the first chirp from a bird she disappeared into the roof eaves. It was amazing how nature had it all worked out. Each animal had his or her moment to sing, hunt, mate, and sleep in a complicated schedule of survival that I only thought about when in the midst of the stillness.

The silence reminded me that I had not heard a peep from Johnson Camp. I wondered how much trouble we were going to be in for our trip across the lake. It was incredibly humid and hot. I got out of bed and threw on the first thing I could find—a dirty tank top from yesterday and a cotton skirt. My flip-flops were by the door, and I slipped them on, tying my hair back as I walked up to Luanne's place.

"Good morning, sunshine," she said from a chair, coffee in hand.

"Can I have a cup?" I moaned. "God, this humidity is awful," I whined.

"Yeah. You know where it is." I was waiting for her to tell me I got her fired, but she didn't say a word.

"I'll row over there and return it," I said when I came back from the cabin with a hot cup of heaven. I would have liked to dump the megaphone in the bear-proof dumpster but didn't want Luanne to get into trouble.

"I'll go with you. Maybe Tom will cut me a break."

"Just stay out of it, Luanne. No one has to know you were there."

"Nah. I don't really give a shit. He shoulda kept her quiet. I've really enjoyed the peace this morning."

We finished our coffee and walked down to get our boats. I stopped in my cabin to grab my paddle and heard Luanne yell, "Oh my God! OH MY GOD!"

I ran down to see what the commotion was. Luanne stood quivering over a woman's body splayed out across the dock. She wore a pink robe in some kind of floral chenille, like an old lady's bed coverlet. It was tattered with rust stains and moth holes. Spindly bluish legs were clad in sagging tube socks on feet that stuck out in opposite directions as if in disagreement over which way to go. Cheap rubber flip-flops clung to them. A headlamp lay on the dock a few feet away, still dimly lit.

It was Emily English.

Her colorless face was turned to one side, her eyes wide open, as if shocked by her condition. I knew that look all too well. She was clearly dead; blood was pooled on the deck around her matted gray hair.

"She's dead, Luanne. Don't touch anything."

"Oh God!" she whispered. Luanne carried the responsibility of camp on her shoulders, and I wondered if she could stand the weight of this.

I looked around to get an idea of what had happened. Emily had obviously suffered a blow to the back of the head. My first thought was a paddle, but fiberglass or plastic paddles weren't going to do it. Even with a wooden paddle it would be tough and take several blows. There was no blood spatter, only a pooling shape from the wound. Luanne began to step closer.

"You'd better get away from there. We're disturbing the scene of the crime."

"Crime? You think someone killed her?"

"Well, she didn't hit herself on the back of the head," I said. "You better go call the police. I'll stay here."

I was a little freaked out about staying with the body by myself. I could imagine her rising up all zombie-like, and groaning, "Use Deet." This wasn't my first experience with the dead, but it's not like you get used to it. I backed away from the body and turned to wait on the shore. There was nothing I could do for her.

I turned around and felt the heel of my rubber flip-flops involuntarily slip on the pool of blood. "Oh shit!" I had just done the very thing I had warned Lu not to do. "Damn it!" I mumbled as I carefully removed my shoe and surveyed the damage. Mine was not the only footprint. I saw that smaller prints had also stepped in the blood, clear and tight footprints without tread marks—probably from flip-flops like mine. I tip-toed with my bloody sandal in one hand, following the other prints off the dock toward the embankment where they disappeared. I took my phone out and snapped a picture of the prints, then left the dock and stuck my flip-flop in the water by the shore.

Luanne came back down the hill with Maddy.

"Oh my God," Maddy said. Luanne had her arm around her, as she looked like she was swaying a little.

"I disturbed the crime scene. What an amateur," I was still rinsing my shoe even though I knew it would never be worn again.

"The police are on their way," Luanne said. The Park Police were at least fifteen miles away. It was going to be a while.

"We were going to return the sound system," Luanne said.

"I have blood on my shoe." I continued to rub it in the grass.

CHAPTER 10

OFFICER LARS CARTER WAS THE first to arrive. He was the hulking stereotype of a meathead cop. There was no doubt that he'd been a football player at some point in his life. His arms were pumped up to the width of his tightly fitting shirt. His hair was cropped closely and added to the already militant look his serious face and rigid posture gave him.

How do you raise such a serious kid? I thought.

"This is Lars Carter," Luanne said, introducing us and quickly puncturing his severe image. "He used to be a lifeguard here."

He didn't look happy about her sharing that information. You could tell he would have preferred to be the authority and not the kid.

"Oh, I remember you, Lars!" Maddy added, which appeared to only make him feel more uncomfortable.

"I'm Lee Harding," I said and reached out to shake his hand. "I stepped in blood," I told him immediately. "I'm sorry."

He took my hand and shook it firmly. "You want to tell me what happened here?" he asked.

I told him how we came upon the body. Luanne would have apprised him already, so I was sure he just wanted to see if our stories matched. I hoped she hadn't said anything about our little robbery the night before, as it was still my intention to get the sound system back to the camp before Tom called the police on us.

It wasn't long before other officers arrived: first a pair of young uniformed men, then an older gentleman who appeared to be in his late fifties. He was about six feet tall but looked small next to Carter. His hair was prematurely white, and he had a kind face with deep roads around the eyes that betrayed a compassionate nature.

"I'm Detective Jed Harris," he said without looking at us. His eyes were on Emily's body and the scene on the dock. "Carter, let's clear the scene," he added, eyes still on the corpse.

"We'll wait up at the pavilion," Luanne responded.

As we walked up the hill, Harris called up to Luanne.

"How many people are currently in camp, ma'am?"

Luanne flipped through her mental list and then answered. "Roz and Moe Martin, Delia Lopez, Randy and Jacob Foster, Bobby Richfield, Therese Azzario, Freddie Papius, Maddy and Henry Levine, plus me, and Lee Harding here. Oh, and Marge Rice and her brother Lester…so fourteen not counting Emily." Her voice cracked a little. The shock was wearing off, and Luanne was starting to feel the darkness of the situation. Finding someone dead is enough to break the strongest person.

The wheels of a car could be heard on the gravel lot. The medical examiner's van had arrived. Detective Harris went to meet him.

Maddy walked quickly toward her cabin to tell Henry the news.

Roz and Moe were coming up the hill.

"What's going on down there?" Moe asked.

"There's been an accident. Can you folks please come with me?" a young officer asked politely and led them to the pavilion.

Carter asked Luanne to escort him to wake the others. She was moving about quickly, like busy work would make things okay, but

I could see that Lu was close to unraveling. Her hands were shaking, and she suddenly appeared frail.

"Give her a minute. She's upset," I told him. "Come on. I'll show you who's here."

He followed me down the narrow path to Delia and Randy's cabin. I knocked on the door, and Delia answered in boxer shorts and a tank top, no bra. She looked at the officer standing behind me, and her expression turned to surprise. I tried to make eye contact so she wouldn't give us away in case she was thinking he was here because of the sound system.

"There's been an accident, Delia. Emily is dead."

"What?" She appeared genuinely shocked.

"Ma'am, I need you all to come up to the pavilion with us right now please," Officer Carter spoke over my shoulder.

"All right. Wow. Okay. Can I just get dressed first? I need to wake the guys."

"Of course, ma'am," Carter said, looking away as if she were naked.

The door to the cabin closed, and I heard rustling and whispers. Randy came to the door in a T-shirt and shorts.

"Emily is dead?" he asked.

"Yeah. She is definitely dead," I answered.

"Wow." He didn't ask how it had happened.

Delia came out dressed in the same tank top (now with a bra) and khaki capris. She and Randy headed up to the pavilion while Carter and I moved down the narrow path toward Therese's cabin, which was a short walk and within view of Randy and Delia's cabin.

Therese was already up and dressed in her lifeguard bathing suit with matching red shorts. I thought I saw a moment of bona fide joy on her face as she recognized Lars Carter from his years on the swim docks, but it faded quickly with the news of Emily's death. In her consistent downbeat way, she closed the door behind her without saying a word and headed up to the pavilion alone.

We walked silently over to the more private side of the peninsula, deeper into the woods, to Bobby's cabin. We stepped over extension cords and firewood to get to the stairs, which were cluttered with logs and a bag of charcoal. His van was in the lot, which meant he was in camp, but no one answered our knock. Bobby was not an early riser.

I opened the door and called his name, knocking on the doorframe again until we heard movement from the bedroom. The living room-kitchen was a mess—dishes piled in the sink and on the counters, clutter everywhere. The odor of a full garbage can filled the room.

Carter looked around the room at the disaster and glanced outside to Bobby's patio where the same chaos reigned. The officer's neat appearance was polar opposite to the chaos that surrounded him.

"Bobby, wake up!" I shouted, feeling like I was trying to get my kids up for school. "Wake up, Bobby!"

"What...I'm up," he finally mumbled. Bobby didn't drink, so I suspected this hangover came from a prescription bottle. Years of chronic pain had dragged him into the whirlpool of addiction.

"It's Lee and Officer Carter. There's been an accident. You need to get up." I could hear him moving. "He's coming," I reassured Carter.

"What's going on?" Bobby asked when he finally wandered out in the clothes he had obviously slept in.

Carter surprised me when he smiled at the mess in front of him.

"Hi, Mr. Richfield," he said with a grin. I should've guessed. Anyone who knew camp knew Bobby.

It took the waking man a moment, but then he smiled back. "Lars! Lars Carter! Well look at you!" He eyed the massive officer from top to bottom. "This guy was the best lifeguard we've ever had at Montego. Don't tell Therese I said that." He chuckled. "Not that I'm not happy to see you, Lars, but uh, what is going on?"

"There's been an accident. One of the campers was found dead this morning," Carter replied.

"Dead? Who?"

"Emily," I replied. I watched his face. He was groggy but showed a numb surprise.

"Emily's dead?" he shook his head. He was thinking about something; I could see it. I couldn't believe no one had asked how. It would have been the first thing out of my mouth.

"We need everyone up at the pavilion." Carter stayed on task.

"All right," he said, digging through the pile of shoes by the door until he found a pair that matched.

We walked back up the narrow path, each of us silent for different reasons. I wondered who would miss Emily. Where was she even from? Did she have any friends or family who would mourn her?

Our next stop was the Rice cabin.

"Emily?" Marge's response to hearing about the woman's death was as cold as a block of ice, but she agreed to comply with Carter's request that she and Lester join the others in the pavilion, all with the air of someone inconvenienced.

The last cabin was Montego, where Freddie stayed. We knocked but no one answered. Since it was a dorm-style residence, it was left unlocked. The cabin was long and narrow, the back wall sharing a wonderful view of the lake on the opposite side of the peninsula from my cabin. The walls were the same aged knotty pine as mine. Shellac applied long ago now crackled. The ceilings were open with cross-beams that did double duty as racks for sailing masts. Old wooden lockers stood in one corner where dozens of paddles were stacked. Another corner was home to a stack of life jackets. In the center was an old table decorated with carved initials and heat stains. A futon served as sofa and overflow bed. A galley kitchen shared a wall with a small bedroom to one side and two curtained doorways to the other.

Carter checked the bedrooms and found them vacant.

"He often paddles late at night and in the morning. He's kind of a loner," I explained to Carter, whose silence made me want to ramble nervously. I knew that Freddie mediated on a tent platform up the hill from Maddy's cabin but didn't say anything. He would turn up, and I was already soaked from walking cabin to cabin in the heat. Neither of us spoke on the way back to the pavilion.

Luanne had made a pot of coffee and was distributing cups to anyone who wanted them. She had pulled herself together admirably. The constant movement was keeping her calm. People seemed agitated, but not distressed. Not one person was crying over the loss of Emily. Therese sat with Roz and Moe. I couldn't help thinking how she'd already lived through a death there—and on the same dock. If the emotions of it were coming back to her, she didn't show it. She looked as aloof as always.

"Folks, we are going to have to wait for Detective Harris to finish up with the medical examiner. Meanwhile, we'll be taking your names and some general information. When the Detective is finished, he'll be interviewing each of you individually," Officer Carter said.

"Are we in danger? Is there a maniac in the park?" asked Moe.

"We don't have those answers yet, sir. At this point I am going to ask you all to stay at camp until further notice."

"Should I close the camp?" Luanne asked.

"Well I certainly wouldn't want anyone else here until our investigation is over," said Carter.

"I'm gonna have to make some calls. I've got people comin' up here this weekend."

"You can go ahead and do that now if you'd like."

Luanne pulled out her cell phone and moved to the corner of the pavilion.

"I can't believe Emily is dead," Randy said in a daze.

"Poor Emily," Roz said.

"Poor Emily was a pain in the ass," I said. "But who would murder her?" I'd opened my mouth just as Detective Harris walked into the pavilion. He wore a faint smile on his face like he found my comments amusing.

"Ma'am, let's you and I start first," he said to me. "The rest of you can wait here until I'm finished. If you need to use the restroom, please ask one of the officers to escort you."

We entered the great room off of the pavilion. It was a large lodge with a huge stone fireplace and an open kitchen. The ceiling was high, the exposed logs proudly showing their strength. An iron chandelier that hadn't worked in decades hung quietly above us. Under different circumstances, the room was typically used for making dinner for events and group gatherings. Sometimes when the weather turned bad, we'd light a fire and play games in here, but otherwise the great space sat empty.

"Jed Harris." He held out his hand and didn't sit down until I did. *A country gentleman,* I thought.

I gave him my name, and he spent a lot of time asking me about my place of residence, family, and occupation. He was warming me up, getting me comfortable talking about myself.

"I take it from your earlier comments that you knew Emily English?" he smiled when he asked me this.

"I only met her two days ago," I said. "The truth is, I don't think anyone here liked Emily much. She was a real pill. But I can't think of why anyone would want to kill her." It was a lie. I'd only known her a couple of days and I'd wanted to throttle her…but not to death. I changed the subject. "Do you deal with a lot of murder in the park?"

"I wouldn't say a lot, no. I've been with Parks for almost forty years. We've found plenty of lost hikers and such. A couple of bodies have been dumped here, the murders taking place somewhere else. It's a shame really, people thrown into the bushes like bags of trash. Mafia dumped a couple of bodies here in the seventies and eighties, but no, I can't say there's been a murder in any of the camps. Montego gets the prize for that one." He was looking out the window of great room, which had an unobstructed view of the swim docks and the lake that sprawled past them. "Had a hiker walk right off a cliff once in a snow storm. That was a real shame."

I looked this kind man over and wondered how the hell he ever became a detective. *He might be out of his element on this one*, I thought.

"Well, I don't really know why, but people have been dying around me for a long time." I thought about my mother lying on her bed, the same color as Emily.

The detective watched me carefully.

I nervously kept talking. "That sounds bad. I lost both of my parents. I actually found my mother in her bed when I was ten years old. Then last year my sister's friend was killed in San Francisco. That was a horror. My sisters and I actually caught the murderer. Well, he almost caught us. Long story."

He cracked a smile. "I would appreciate any help you could give me now. Where were you last night?"

"When?" I asked.

"We don't have the exact time of death yet. Just tell me about your night."

"I had dinner at Roz and Moe's with Maddy, Henry, Freddie, and Luanne. Then a bunch of us went for a night swim…and a few of us went for a paddle." I added that last part with a lump in my throat.

"A moonlight paddle," he said in a kind of faraway voice. Was he a romantic? The park was a great place for romantics, though it seemed at odds with his job.

"Yes, we took the war canoe over to Johnson Camp and back. There has been some unruly noise over there, and we wanted to talk to Tom Johnson about it."

"I see. A paddle with a purpose." He cracked a smile. "And did you? Talk to Tom?"

"Yes. We spoke to him." I thought about the incident on the beach, Tom in his wet shorts. "Then we came back here and I went to bed. I'd had a full day of swimming and paddling yesterday and slept pretty hard."

"So you didn't see or hear anything unusual?"

"Not a thing. My cabin is the closest to the scene, Detective. Just a hundred yards down the path. I'm sorry I don't have more to give you." Thoughts of the sound system that was stashed in the war canoe flooded my mind, turning my face red with guilt.

"Well, if you see or hear anything suspicious, let me know," he said, handing me his card.

I felt his eyes on my hot face and turned an even darker shade of scarlet. I was a terrible liar. "We don't get cell phone reception here. Will you be around for the next few days? What if this was some crazy serial killer hanging out in the woods, like *Friday the Thirteenth*?"

"Unlikely." He smiled, and I wasn't sure if it was kindness or condescension. "But there will be a police presence until we get some answers."

I got up to leave, sensing the conversation was over.

Harris called Bobby in as I left. The man looked like a disaster in yesterday's clothes. His thin hair was stuck to his head. I could smell his morning breath when he walked by—or maybe that was my own hung-over stench.

CHAPTER 11

I WALKED STRAIGHT OUT OF the pavilion to see Luanne. Thoughts of my parents' deaths filled my head. Why couldn't Emily be the one to have an aneurism? She had no children. No family. Why had *both* of my parents been taken so early? I knew life was unfair. I'd known of a couple that had lost all three of their children in a mudslide. All three kids in one horrible rainy night. *There are no answers.*

My memories of my parents were limited, especially with my father, who died when I was eight years old. He was sick for two years before that, so there were a lot of hushed moments in the house so we wouldn't disturb him. My mother tried hard to make things normal for us. My sisters, who were both almost a decade older than me, couldn't rebel like normal teenagers and instead became burdened with a premature sense of responsibility for my mother. I became the quiet child, trying to stay out of the way. When he finally died, the house went silent—no laughter at meals, no music to sway to, only rooms thick with grief.

Some time later, my mother sat us down and read us a letter from our father. She said it took her three months to be able to read it out loud, but that is what he had asked her to do. I still have a copy, even though I know it by heart.

My Dear Girls,

Leaving you has been the hardest thing I've ever done. It's unbearable and cruel and unfair. All of the emotions that you are feeling now are right and true. Feel them, and then let them go. Don't look for reasons why this happened. There are no answers.

In front of you is the great adventure of life. Your life! Honor what you have; your mother, your birthplace (you hit the lottery), the freshness of the air, the height of the trees. Rejoice in being alone, in freedom. Ferociously feed your minds. Be kind and work hard at what you love to do. Don't rely on anyone but yourself, but share in your partnership generously. In the end, I hope you can look into the eyes of someone you love, as I was able to, and be grateful that you had this lifetime, however long it is.

It's time to move on. You carry me with you.

Your Loving Father,
Ben

Two years later, on a school day, I woke up on my own. My sisters were away at college, and the house was eerily quiet. I checked the kitchen, where my mother usually sat drinking her coffee and grading papers. No one was there. I eventually found her in her bedroom, lying on her side, never rising with the light of day. Even at ten years of age, I knew that the purplish-gray hue of her skin was wrong. After I called 911, I crawled into her bed and pleaded with her to come back. I touched her cold skin and begged God and my father to make her come back. It's my most vivid memory of my mother.

There are no answers. Sometimes my father's words rang true. Sometime they didn't.

CHAPTER 12

LUANNE WAS MAKING HER LAST call when I got to her cabin. I waited on the seat of the picnic table, which sat in the dirt on the downside of the hill, facing the lake. It was so quiet in camp that I could hear cars from the park road more than a mile away.

Emily's death had been a distraction from my own sorry affairs. For some reason it had removed the anger and frustrations I'd been feeling about my marriage and replaced them with sorrow. *Was my family dying too?*

Luanne's little dwelling was the only one with cell phone reception, thanks to a booster on her roof. If you stood under her kitchen window—on one leg with one hand in the air and sideways—you could get one bar on your phone. Other campers had figured this out, and she told me she'd often heard people making calls under her window as she lay in her bed at night.

I never used the spot unless it was an emergency. This felt like one of those times. I wandered over to the window and stood on the rock someone had strategically placed there. When a single bar appeared, I dialed Jack's office number.

"Hey," I said when he answered.

"Hey yourself. I've tried calling you about ten thousand times. Thanks for calling me back." He was obviously angry.

"I wasn't ready," I said in a whisper that was going to bring tears very soon.

"What? I can barely hear you."

"I wasn't ready," I said a little louder. It lost its tenderness and sounded snotty. "You're not going to believe what I am about to tell you."

"What?" I don't know what he was expecting me to say, but it wasn't anything like what I was about to tell him. There was anger and hurt in his voice.

My heart was breaking. All of the pain of the last few months rushed in like a flash flood. Pain I had been so good at forgetting since I got here. *Fucking Emily*, I thought uncharitably. *She ruined my retreat.* "Someone died on the docks," I told him.

"I can barely hear you. Did you say someone died on the rocks?"

"SOMEONE WAS KILLED HERE. LUANNE AND I FOUND THE BODY!" I yelled. I am sure they could hear me at the pavilion. Luanne looked down at me from the window.

"What do you mean 'killed?' Like an accident?"

"Nope," I replied. He had to be getting used to it by now. I started laughing. It was a ridiculous, emotional, and completely out of control crazy woman laugh. "No, a woman was murdered," I spit out as my laughter turned to crying, real crying.

Luanne came out and put her arms around me. She probably thought I was crying about Emily's death, but it really wasn't about her. She took the phone out of my hands and walked into her cabin. I heard her explaining things to Jack. I walked back over to the picnic table and cried some more. It felt so good to get it out.

"I don't think they'll let you in, Jack," I heard Luanne say. A little while later, she ended the call and came back out and sat across from me. She handed me the phone. I straightened up. I felt really stupid for breaking.

"I had no idea you felt so deeply for Emily," she said.

We both let out guilty little chuckles, but it turned to true sadness as we both found ourselves with tears running down our faces, this time for the poor old woman who'd died. Once things settled down, Luanne brought me a cup of coffee, and we sat in her chairs whispering about the previous night. Bobby came down from his interview, and I saw Officer Carter escorting Moe to the restrooms.

"So Moe needs an escort to the bathroom, but we can walk around freely?" I asked Bobby.

"Yeah, and let's face it, if someone outside of camp did this, they are long gone already anyway," Luanne said.

"It had to be someone from outside camp. No one here would do that," Bobby said.

"Anyone is capable of murder, Bobby. Trust me. They should be looking for a motive," I said. I was surprised when Bobby didn't reply with, "I could never murder someone." I would have thought he would say it, and I would have probably had a hard time believing otherwise. I wasn't surprised that Luanne wouldn't say it. She always talked about killing people. Not literally, but wanting to in a general way.

"I think they may be a little out of their league," Bobby said.

"You think?" I replied.

"The detective never even asked me about my relationship with Emily," he added.

"How was your relationship?" I asked.

"She was a miserable bitch," he said flatly.

"Wow, Bobby. I didn't know you had it in you."

"You think she thanked me when I put her screen back on? No. She said, 'If I get West Nile because it took you so long, I'm holding you responsible.'"

"Yeah, there was a reason she was alone," Luanne added.

"Not exactly motive for someone to treat her like a whac-a-mole though, right?" It wasn't a question really, but I could see in both of my friends' eyes that there was more. Instead of delving into it, though, Bobby hobbled off to his cabin.

"I saw the inside of his place this morning," I confided to Luanne.

"He's a fuckin' slob," she stated.

Maddy and Henry came down the hill and stopped to talk. "Let's go out for breakfast. You guys want to go to the Road House?" Maddy suggested.

"Yes!" I said. "Let me get some shoes." I had thrown my tainted flip-flops in the dumpster. "Come on, Luanne. I'm taking you to breakfast, and I don't want to hear a thing about how you need to stay here."

"Think they're gonna let us go?" she asked.

"We aren't under arrest. Come on, get up, you're going."

"All right. All right." She grabbed her bag, and we headed down to my place. We didn't say it out loud, but none of us wanted to be alone.

I looked at Emily's cabin on the way down. Luanne had the key to every cabin in camp.

"Should we go lock Emily's place up?" I said. "Maybe there's evidence in there."

"Might not be a bad idea," she said as we changed course and headed over to Emily's. Just as we approached the stairs, Bobby came out of the cabin, as surprised to see us as we were to see him.

"Hey," he said, looking down at us from the stair deck.

"Hey," I answered.

"What were you doin' in there, Bobby?" Luanne had no patience for him.

"I was gonna make sure everything was turned off and lock it up," he said, but he looked like he was lying; his face was bright red.

"Yeah, I got it," Luanne said and pushed past him. She opened the door first as if to make sure he had done what he said.

"Jeez, it looks like your place, Bobby. What a mess," she said.

Bobby walked the path to his cabin with his hands on his hips, as if to hold his aching back in place.

"That was awkward," I whispered when I was sure Bobby was out of range.

"He thinks he runs this place," Luanne said.

I popped my head into the cabin from the stairs. "What the…? It's trashed!"

There were clothes tossed about everywhere and the kitchen counter was full of contents from the cabinets. It looked like a very disorganized person was packing to move.

"Not our problem," Luanne said, shutting the door and locking it.

"Do you think Bobby did that?" I asked her.

"Not our problem. Come on, I'm hungry," she said, walking away.

It was 10:00 a.m. when we pulled out of camp in Maddy and Henry's SUV. I would have rather been out paddling this morning, but instead I was thinking about what lay on the aluminum dock where I had watched so many sunsets.

"My kids still talk about Therese's brother dying on that rock. Everyone knows what happened there, and that was forty-five years ago. Imagine how they are going to feel about the spot now," Maddy said sadly, looking down the hill toward the scene that was hidden from us by the woods.

"Hey, Maddy, I brought you a present." I tossed her a cannabis caramel. I always had a stash for museums, concerts, and long walks in the woods. They slowed me down and created an enhanced experience. Today they were used to escape.

"Don't I get one?" Henry asked.

"These are 'special' caramels from Lee's sister in California, honey. You're designated driver."

It was hard to get weed on the East Coast. My sister had a medicinal license in California (for PMS). She sent me care packages regularly.

"Oh," he said, and then after a pause, "Oooh! Got it."

Luanne ignored us. Like Jack, she frowned upon stoners like Maddy and me; Patrick, Lu's husband, had had a problem with drugs early on in their marriage, so her opinion of the habit was low.

Patrick was a friendly guy with opinions about everything from how to build a floating dock to how to pick winning stocks...only he'd never built anything, his finances were a disaster, and the only thing that kept him from regular DUIs was the fact that his license had been revoked due to priors. Luanne didn't allow him to drive her minivan since he had already crashed one family car. He was currently working as a bartender at the corner dive by their house.

There at the gate, which was closed, was a police car.

"Wait until we get past this guy, Maddy," I suggested. "They smell when you open them."

"We're just heading out to get some breakfast," Henry told the officer when we pulled up to the gate. The young cop opened the gate after glancing into the backseat and then closed it after us.

"Jesus! We could have been smuggling the killer out. Or the murder weapon!" Luanne said.

"If there is a murder weapon around, I'm sure it's at the bottom of the lake somewhere already," I pointed out. But the more I thought about it, the more unsure I was. There were branches, paddles, and firewood all over the camp. It could have been burned. And what about Tom's strange behavior? If he did it, the weapon could be anywhere between here and Johnson Camp...

I decided to eat my caramel and not think about it for a while.

We chose to sit at a round table on the back deck. It had a large umbrella for shade and a red checked tablecloth. The deck overlooked the beach and creek. You could see that someone had had a bonfire recently.

The Bloody Marys at Earl's Road House were served in a half carafe with a long piece of celery for stirring, some pickled string beans, olives, and the longest straw I'd ever seen. I had two, and the pot caramel had kicked in with a wave of undying calm.

I had to walk through the bar to get to the restrooms. Earl's was always busy, and even on this weekday morning, there were customers around the large bar. A moose head had a woman's bra hanging from it, something I hadn't noticed last time I was there. It was small and lacy and wasn't purchased for its supportive qualities. "Werewolf of London" played too loudly for that particular morning.

I noticed Tom Johnson sitting at the bar, thinking deeply over a freshly poured beer. He looked up, and I tried to pretend that I hadn't seen him, but he caught my eye. I looked twice and acted surprised, nodded hello with my chin, then rushed off to the restroom.

"Shit. Shit. Shit," I whispered to myself. Afterwards, I walked out the front door of the restaurant, hoping Tom would think I was leaving, and then went around the back gate up to the deck. I thought I was being very clever, but when I came up the stairs to the deck, Tom was standing at the table talking to the others.

"Hi, Tom," I said in a resigned tone.

"Tom was just telling us how there was a problem in his camp last night. Apparently someone stole his guests' megaphone and amp," Henry told me with a look that said, "shh."

"Really?" I said without heart. I am a terrible liar and could not help but feel sorry for this guy. I wished I wasn't so stoned, or that he wasn't there, so I could enjoy it more.

"Listen, guys, I am really sorry about the noise. You can't believe what it's been like. Joan took the kids to her mother's. She couldn't take it anymore. This is not the first time this summer that I've sat at the bar at 10 a.m.," he confessed like a broken man.

"Why don't you pull up a seat and join us for breakfast, Tom?" Maddy said.

The rest of us looked at her like she was insane.

"Naw. Thanks. I really appreciate that, but I have to get back. I told them I was filing a police report at Park headquarters. I came here instead."

"All the police are over at our camp anyway, Tom," I said.

He stared blankly at me.

"You guys didn't tell him?" I asked the others.

"Tell me what?" Tom asked.

"Emily English was found dead this morning," Luanne said.

One of Tom's eyebrows went up and the other stayed down. "Dead? Dead-dead?" he asked.

"Yeah. Dead-dead."

"Do they know who did it?"

Why do you think someone "did it"? I was about to ask, but Henry opened his big mouth first.

"No, but they questioned everyone this morning. They might come over to you guys too I guess. Not like she made any friends your way."

"Hey, we were happy to see her cross the lake, but I can't imagine why anyone would want to kill her." Tom said his goodbyes and headed out.

"How did he know she was murdered?" I asked out loud when he left.

No one else seemed to think it was odd.

"She could have slipped and fell. Or died in her sleep. God knows she had enough ailments," I insisted, but no one was listening to me. They were reading their menus, and the conversation turned to food.

I wasn't interested in eating. I wondered if Emily's dead body was still lying on the dock and if it would smell soon or if fish were eating her blood. Did that mean that if you caught that fish, you'd be eating Emily English? I guessed it was no different than if a person was cremated and their ashes thrown into the ocean. We were all returned to the earth one way or another.

"I wonder if Roz and Moe will stay," Luanne mused.

"This must be weird for Therese. It must bring up memories of her brother's death," Maddy said.

I thought about my boys, away at camp with all those other rough-housings boys. I had a moment of sheer terror. You just never know in life. The odds of avoiding more tragedy didn't go down just because my parents had died young. That's not how it worked. "I would curl up and die if I lost one of my kids," I said.

"No you wouldn't," Luanne said matter-of-factly. "You'd have to survive for the other child."

Everyone at the table was a parent, so there was thoughtful silence as we tried not to imagine the unimaginable.

With my morning buzz came the emotions alcohol often pushes to the top. I missed my kids. My family was falling apart. "I need to make a call, you guys. I'll be back before breakfast gets here," I said as I stood up and walked down to the beach below the deck. I planted myself in a bright red Adirondack chair and dialed the number that I always call when I feel like crying or when something goes wrong or somebody pisses me off—my sister Alice.

"Hey, Dummy. Where the hell have you been?" she answered. She's always called me "Dummy" affectionately.

"Hey. I'm up at the lake. I have no reception here, remember?"

"Well, you better call Lacy. She's freaking out."

I rolled my eyes. Our older sister Lacy was like the mother I no longer had, which included worrying about me like I was a child.

"Guess what?" I told Alice.

"What?"

"This old lady was murdered at camp."

"Shut up!"

"I kid you not. Dead on the docks."

"Did you kill her?"

"Shut up! Like I really need this right now. I came here to get away, you know?"

"Poor sister." Alice was great at feeling bad for me, which I really needed right now. "Seriously though, Lee, just get the hell out of there. You don't need this. What if it's some kook like in that horror movie?" She proceeded to make "tttttt hahahaha tttttt hahahah" noises like in *Friday the Thirteenth*.

I'd thought about this. Leaving would be the smart thing to do. But I didn't want to leave Luanne, and I knew she wasn't going anywhere. And then there was the real reason I wouldn't leave camp. "I don't want to go home." I started crying. Alice knew exactly what had been going on for the past few months. She'd listened to me go from ranting and angry to tenderly sad and back at least fifteen times. "Fucking murderer fucked up my trip," I sobbed. We both laughed, and I felt better for the moment. "I'm on my second Bloody Mary at Earl's. And a caramel."

"I can tell. You have a fat tongue. Don't go back to camp, please, sister." I understood her concern but had no intention of honoring her request.

"I'm okay. Really. I am with my lake friends, and we'll stick together."

We said our love-you-and-goodbyes, and I dried my eyes and headed back to the table. Luanne could see I'd been crying but didn't say anything. She always knew what was going on. Henry was just Henry. He is classic man. I could cry at the table, and he wouldn't say anything. Not because he didn't care, but because he just wouldn't know what to say.

Like me, Maddy was baked out of her mind and on her second drink. Our food came while she told us a story about how she had met Emily. She forgot what she was talking about mid-story, and I was right there with her. When I tried reminding her of what she had forgotten, we both started laughing. Then we were ridiculously snorting and crying while Henry chuckled and Luanne just shook her head.

The burdens of my life slipped off my shoulders like a heavy shawl, and I didn't bend over to pick them up.

CHAPTER 13

I CAN'T SAY THERE WAS excitement about going back to camp, but there wasn't dread either. Camp would be abuzz, and it was still mid-week. There would be nothing dull about the coming days.

The same cop who let us out was standing guard at the gate when we came back.

"How long are you going to be here?" I asked from the back seat.

"I don't know, ma'am. As long as it takes I guess."

I really hated when people called me ma'am. I guess I would have preferred miss, or even lady, to ma'am. I was no longer a miss though, which made me a little sad.

"If someone wants to get in or out of camp without being seen, don't you think they will just walk through the woods?" I asked him.

"I'm just doing my job, ma'am." He looked like he was sixteen years old, and I felt like a bully for making him uncomfortable.

I shook my head and laughed as Henry drove along the winding camp road. The lake below crackled with light against the brilliance of the mossy green forest. Ancient schist rose jagged from the earth, pushed out by glaciers. This rock was some of the oldest on earth. The stone could be ankle breaking for hikers, especially in the fall when the leaves covered them up.

I thought about the Redwoods I'd grown up around and wished I could show them to Luanne and Maddy. Describing a tree with a two-hundred-foot circumference was impossible. The sequoia had to be experienced in order for one to learn how really insignificant one was. I knew Luanne would never see them. Her life in Brooklyn was financially difficult. Giving her kids more than she could afford meant a simple existence for herself. The lake would be as far as she ever traveled.

Moments later we pulled onto the gravel parking lot in the center of camp. The medical examiner had gone, taking Emily away to a refrigerated drawer, the next leg of her journey. Two dusty cop cars were parked on the shady side of the lot, but no one was about.

After thanking Henry for driving, I started the walk down to my cabin—not without a little bit of a sway. I looked back at Emily's place and saw a figure peer out from the front door. It was Officer Carter, looking to see who was approaching. I changed directions and headed over to Emily's.

"Did you guys find a murder weapon yet?" I asked.

"Can't say, ma'am."

"Please call me Lee, okay?"

"Sure, ma'am...Lee."

He reminded me of my nephew Andrew, Alice's son. He's a serious guy like Carter. I don't really know how we got such a serious kid in our crazy family, but we had two. My older son Jack Jr. was the same way. I called him John Cotton sometimes because of his predisposition to the hard line. He was our own little puritan. And then there was my sister Lacy...okay, maybe it was in the blood after all.

Detective Harris stepped out of the cabin.

"Hello, Ms. Harding," he said kindly, like he was genuinely happy to see me again.

"Hi, Detective. I was just coming back to my cabin but saw you over here. Thought I would see if you needed anything. How are things coming along?"

"Well, the autopsy will tell us more about what she was struck with. But we have a pretty good idea of what happened. Ms. Harding here is a veteran at this, Carter. She's solved a murder before." He nodded to Carter as if to reassure him that it was true. Carter didn't appear to find it impressive.

"Please call me Lee. And I didn't solve the murder. I'm just good at earning people's trust. As an old friend of mine tells me, 'You'd talk to a lamppost.' It's true; I like to talk to people, and sometimes they tell me things." I spoke quickly when I was nervous. I said this too fast. Carter was probably thinking I was nuts, or the murderer. Either way he just stared at me. "I think people deserve answers. That's all. Don't you?"

Carter nodded at me from the stairs, where he stood blocking the door like I was an uninvited guest.

"Her cabin is a mess, right?" I said. "I saw it with Luanne earlier, but we didn't go inside."

"Yeah. I'm trying to figure out if someone went through it or if it always looked like this," Harris said.

I considered telling him about Bobby's visit but didn't have the heart to betray him, not yet anyway. "Judging by the condition of her car, I'd say she was messy. It looks like she lived in it," I said.

Emily's early 1980s sedan was parked outside of the cabin. Its peeling vinyl roof and oxidized silver paint reminded me of Emily— tired and abandoned and desperate to keep going. There was so much garbage in the back seat that you couldn't see the floor. Empty fast food drink cups and papers and a towel that looked like it had mopped up more than one mess and would hold its crunchy shape all mixed together in a forgotten shallow pool. The front was pretty much in the same condition, except for the driver's seat, which had an inflatable pillow resting on it.

"It's weird. She didn't come off like a messy person. She was so particular about the rules," I said.

"Maybe she was so busy watching others, she didn't have time for her own rules. Maybe that's what got her killed," Harris replied.

He was pretty smart for a dummy. Maybe I had him wrong. "So you think she knew something she wasn't supposed to?" I asked but then remembered something. "'I know lots of secrets around here,'" I said out loud.

"You do?" Harris asked me, looking puzzled.

"No, no. That's what Emily told me yesterday. I thought it was weird, but then she was a weird woman."

"Well I guess we're going to have to figure out some of her secrets, aren't we?" he directed this at me.

"We?" I asked him, pointing my fingers at myself. Carter looked at him like he was insane.

"Look, you're here, and I could use your help if you'll give it. I hear you did a fine job in San Francisco."

"What?" I wanted to die. "How did you…?"

"You didn't think we wouldn't check our facts now did you? My officer back at the station called the SFPD. All we had to do was mention your name and a Detective Healy there spoke very highly of you. Said we'd be lucky to have your help."

I blushed at the thought of Detective Erik Healy. We'd gotten close during my time in San Francisco—close enough for me to occasionally still wonder what could have been.

Harris was watching me. I wanted to fan my hot face.

"I had a psychic help me once. Missing person's case. Older lady went for a walk in the park and vanished. She had the early stages of Alzheimer's. Some of the family members thought maybe she committed suicide. Psychic walks in and tells us the lady's fine; she's living by the beach in Florida in a house with a blue door and the number seven in the address. Turned out the woman had a lover for two decades, and when she got sick, he picked her up and they disappeared down to Florida. The boyfriend sent her back six months later when she couldn't remember his name."

"So what was their address?" I asked.

"White door, address was one twenty-six. Multiple of seven." He smiled and winked.

I laughed. "I'd be happy to help you in any way I can. Just so you know, though, I have no psychic powers."

"Just let me know if you hear or see anything that might help us figure this out, okay?"

I agreed then said my goodbyes and headed toward the restrooms. All those drinks had caught up to me, and by the time I got there, it was an emergency situation. I opened the door too quickly.

Delia was standing at the sink. "Hi, Lee," she said.

I blew past her and then came back out again when I realized there was no toilet paper in the first two stalls. I opened a rustic corner cabinet and peered into the neatly stocked shelves. The top shelf was filled with toilet paper rolls, and on the middle shelf there were paper towels. On the bottom sat a few containers of liquid hand soap and a roll of packing tape. I remembered that Emily had been the one responsible for bathroom duty this week.

In the front of the building was a unisex room for washing. A large trough sink lined one wall and a laundry station lined another. The mirrors were old and had black spots forming behind them like fungus. I looked at my puffy eyes and bed head with disappointment. I'd assumed the ponytail had helped, but it hadn't.

Delia was still there. I had the feeling she was looking for someone to talk to.

I looked in the mirror again and groaned. "I have a hangover," I confessed. "Bloody Marys for breakfast."

Delia's eyes widened a little, and she shook her head in understanding. "I could use a drink right now," she said. "We don't keep anything in the cabin because of Jacob."

"I have bourbon and wine in my cabin if you need them."

"I may take you up on the bourbon," she said, surprising me. I'd had her pegged as a white wine drinker. Maybe even a wine cooler if they still made those. "I just can't believe Emily's dead," she said.

"I know. I don't think it's really sunk in for me yet either. Were the two of you close?"

She laughed. "Close? The woman was a viper."

I was surprised. Delia was so tolerant; she lived with Randy, a man who talked just to hear his own voice. Emily must have been even worse than I thought.

"Did anyone care for that woman?" I asked.

"Not that I know of."

"But who would dislike her enough to kill her?" I asked.

She struggled for a moment, but it didn't feel genuine to me. She had waited around to get something off her mind. Sweet Delia wanted to gossip. Well, Detective Harris *wanted* me to listen to gossip, so I was all ears.

"Do you know something, Delia? If you do, you should share it."

She feigned hesitation. "I was walking down the steps to the dock yesterday to take my morning swim. I heard arguing and it stopped me. I didn't want to interrupt anything, you know? So I stood there a moment to hear who it was. Therese was on duty. Actually, Jacob was supposed to be there with her, but he'd slept in again," she frowned and I could see the frustration in her face.

"Anyway, Therese and Emily were having quite the argument. They were really going at it. It was a shame because the mist was still on the lake and I love to swim when it's like that, but I had no intention of barging in on them."

"What were they arguing about?"

"I have no idea. I didn't stay to find out."

"You didn't hear *anything*?" I asked incredulously.

"I just heard Therese say, 'You have no right! You have no right to intrude like that!' I've never heard her so mad. Well, she's always kinda mad, but quietly mad, you know?"

I nodded. "What do you think Emily was intruding on?" I asked.

"Who knows? She was an intruder with a capital I."

I thought about how she'd ruined my swim the other day. "Yes, she was," I agreed.

We walked out of the restrooms together, and I waved goodbye as I headed to my cabin for a nap. I thought about the last time I had seen Emily, how she'd been on her way into the bathroom with cleaning supplies. She had a bandana on her head like she was someone's maid. I thought again of Carol Burnett. I smiled and decided that, even though I hadn't liked Emily, I would be the one to mourn her. What the hell, I was a mess anyway.

CHAPTER 14

I TOOK THE BEST NAP of my life. I was too drunk to dream and too stoned to be worried about anything. The sound of the woods woke me gently some time later. Squirrels ran across my roof, and something rustled in the leaves outside the window of my bedroom. I heard a voice yelling to another from far away, echoing until it disappeared. Birds crooned their love songs through the treetops, and the dragonflies hunted in a low hum over the water.

They say that moment of sleep to wake is a moment of nirvana. Birth was also one, death another. But so were sneezes, orgasms, and the seconds right *before* falling asleep. A nap allowed for one to wake slowly and without the startling buzz of an alarm. I was incredibly present for a few minutes, my body completely relaxed. I stared up at the knots in the pine ceiling, thinking of nothing and everything.

A hard crunch of leaves brought me back to reality. Maybe it was a deer? Maybe not. I felt a stab of fear. Someone had been murdered last night, and like in a bad teen movie, I was in the woods waiting to be the next victim. My fear turned to anger. I loved this peaceful place. I'd never been afraid of anything but spiders. And water snakes. And ticks and bears. And what lay at the dark bottom of the lake. I'd been scared of many things, but not murderers.

"Shit," I groaned as I stood up and stretched. I had no idea what time it was. I looked out the window and through the trees down to the lake. The sun was shining on the water, but the shoreline was shaded, telling me it was late in the afternoon. A canoe paddled in the distance, slow in the heat of the July day. Somewhere on the lake, beavers rested in the cool shade of their dens, their own waking hour coming soon. I touched my neck and felt the dampness of my skin, extremely aware of the slow sensuality of the hot summer afternoon.

I could have stood there for some time, staring mindlessly into the depth of the lake, but the yellow caution tape on the dock reminded me of the day's events, and I reluctantly left the cabin to see what had transpired while I'd been checked out. No one was in front of Luanne's cabin. I heard talking coming from the pavilion, so I headed that direction.

"He wasn't rich exactly, but had money. I remember once he bought Jake a battery-operated..." Randy was droning on. He often told detailed stories about people you didn't know or care about. He was like a grating song in a place where I didn't have permission to change the station.

Luanne was playing cards with Maddy and Randy at one of the tables in the pavilion. It was decked out camp style with a red-checkered tablecloth and stacks of tall jewel-toned aluminum cups. A large thermos sat close to Lu. The light from the open walls lit their game, surrounding the space with authentic forest wallpaper with the exception of the wall with the large stone fireplace, which seemed to mock us in the heat. Randy was in the midst of a story that I guessed did not have a beginning, middle, or end. I heard something about his great uncle George.

"Hey there, sleepin' beauty," Luanne said, interrupting him.

"How'd you know I was sleeping?" I asked.

Luanne and Maddy looked at each other and laughed.

"'Cause we were bangin' on your cabin door. We thought you were dead. I used my key just to make sure you weren't. Sorry." Luanne's eyes hit the floor in shame. She was big on privacy.

"It's fine, Luanne. Thanks for caring," I reassured her.

"I made her do it," Maddy said. "We knew you were alive 'cause you were snoring like a bear."

"Hey, you never slept?" I asked Maddy.

"No, Luanne wouldn't let me. She's been pumping me up with coffee since we got back. Still enjoying that candy you gave me. Now I'm both mellow and hyper."

Luanne rolled her eyes, and Randy looked confused. Poor Luanne. If anyone needed an induced escape, she did. She just wouldn't go there. "Yeah, thanks, Lee. I've sat here all afternoon with a drooling vegetable," Luanne said.

"Shut up," Maddy said with a smile on her face.

"Are the police still here?" I asked, changing the subject so Randy didn't have time to ask what we were talking about. Luanne motioned for me to sit down.

"They're headquarted up in the great room. Doesn't look like they're going anywhere," Randy replied before Luanne could speak. "Forensics has been here all afternoon. One of the guys that was here grew up on the same street as my uncle in Staten Island. Can you believe that? It's such a small world. They even went to the same elementary school, not at the same time; my uncle was five years older than him. He knew—"

"That's good," I interrupted, addressing Luanne. If I didn't, Randy would never have stopped. "I was afraid they were going to leave us here with a murderer."

She shrugged and rolled her eyes again. "I don't have any great expectations about their abilities. They're country police. This guy's never investigated a murder. And that Carter kid is like a giant robot. He was like that as a kid too. 'Go to the water and get the body,'" she said in an Arnold Schwarzenegger slash Brooklyn accent that made me laugh.

"That's not good," I added.

"He asked me if any boats were missing. Like maybe Emily had come across a boat-thieving ring. Why the hell would a boat thief fuck up her cabin?" The head shaking and eye rolling began again. People just annoyed Luanne.

"So her cabin was trashed? She wasn't just a slob?" I asked.

"She *was* a slob. I've been in that cabin," said Randy.

"Why were you in Emily's cabin?" I asked. I couldn't see her inviting him over for tea.

"I was thinking about entering the lottery for the cabin by the outhouses. The guy who has it now is never there. I was going to ask him if I could take over his lease. When I mentioned it to Emily, she said I should come over to her place first. She said, when the wind blows, her patio smells bad."

I believed it. The outhouses were once the only bathrooms in the camp. They were in a rustic-style building that had an open porch with sinks. We still used the two stalls when we were on that side of camp, but the eye-watering smell of chemicals and crap made us hold our breath on certain days.

"So I went over. I'd never seen that cabin, so she let me have a look. It was a mess. Dishes were piled up, and clothes and papers were everywhere."

Randy would've continued to talk, but Luanne cut in. "Yeah, but someone was lookin' for somethin' in that cabin. Things were turned upside down. It wasn't just messy. Boat thief my ass."

I could see her point. "So you're entering the lottery?" I asked Randy.

"Yeah, it's time. I'm tired of hauling my stuff back and forth each time we come up."

"How many people are in the lottery this year, Lu?"

She took a moment to think about it. "Only six. Randy and Dal, Emily, the Smyths—but they don't stand a chance; they're never here and haven't done anything around camp." Campers must do a certain amount of community service to get a cabin. "And then there are the regular lease holders: Moe and Roz, Therese, and the Rices."

"And how many cabins' leases are up?" I asked her.

"Three," she said without having to think about it. It was a big deal—the thing that had everyone tense. "All the regulars."

This was why we didn't go for a lease. Which of these old-timer's cabins could I go after? There was no way I'd want Moe and Roz to lose their cabin. And Therese was an institution. Her family was one of the originals. So were the Rices, and I'd heard that their cabin was supposedly completely remodeled. Anyone would want it, but I just couldn't get wrapped up in that.

"So which cabin did Emily want?" I asked.

"I don't know," Luanne replied.

"Does anyone?"

"Beats me," she answered.

Would someone kill a woman over a cabin lease? "How is Jacob taking the news?" I asked Randy. I was so happy my boys weren't up here at this time.

"He's been sleeping all day. He wasn't feeling well."

"He wasn't in the pavilion this morning?" Luanne's eyes were wide open in disbelief.

"He's sick, the poor kid," Randy replied.

"He shoulda been there, Randy. Sick or not." Luanne frowned. She headed up to the pavilion to tell Harris. Maddy and I followed.

"It's not like he had anything to do with it. Why are you making such a big deal about it?" he yelled after us. He was still sitting alone at the table when we left, looking like he'd been made to wear the dunce cap.

I wanted to talk to Harris but didn't want Luanne or Maddy to know about our agreement. No one would tell me anything if they thought it would get to the police. I hoped he wouldn't blow my cover.

When we entered the great room off the pavilion I was surprised. The officers had pulled some of the folding tables we use for potluck dinners together to make a square desk in the center of the room. There were already stacks of files, two laptops, and two walkie-talkies lying on the table. The detective was speaking to someone on the walkie-talkie and motioned for us to come in.

"Just put it on your own card, Stevens. I'll pay you back myself," he said into the device and then set it down. "Hello, ladies. I'm working on getting a booster up here so I can get a better signal for our phones and laptops. You should be able to use your own phones too. It's a win–win." He smiled his gentle country smile, and I realized that his game was good.

"Hello, Detective," I said. "Nice setup here," I gave him an "I know what you're up to" smile. "What's all the paperwork?" I asked.

"I've got all kinds of stuff here, thanks to Parks and Luanne Murphy."

"Yeah, that's why we're here. I missed something this morning." Luanne was taking responsibility for Randy's bad behavior. "There's a teenager still sleepin' in one of the cabins."

Harris tilted his head a little when he looked at her and waited for more.

"Randy Foster's kid, Jacob. He's been up here trainin' to be a lifeguard. He's sick or something, so Randy didn't wake him up this morning."

"Randy and Delia didn't wake him up," I added. "I should have noticed too, when I went down there with Officer Carter. Sorry," I added.

Harris looked at his watch. "It's two thirty in the afternoon."

"He's a spoiled brat," Maddy added. "They cater to his every whim. I'll bet they were too afraid of him to wake him."

"Thanks for the information, ladies. Lee, would you mind showing me where the cabin is? I have a couple more questions for you anyway, and we can talk on the way."

Luanne's eyebrows scrunched together. "What the—?" I could practically hear them saying.

"I'll be needing to talk with you again also, Mrs. Murphy. Where can I find you?"

The brows relaxed a little, and Luanne told him she'd be in front of her cabin.

"I already told you I didn't do it, Officer," I joked.

No one laughed.

"I'm okay, you guys. Don't worry. Jeez." It was like having my sisters around. Luanne and Maddy left reluctantly.

"Carter, could you please find Mr. and Mrs. Foster and ask them to wait for me here?" Harris said.

"Randy and Delia aren't married," I reminded him.

"Oh yeah, right. Okay, find Mr. Foster and Msssss…what was her name, Carter?"

Carter looked as his notepad for a moment then replied, "Lopez."

"Yes. Ms. Lopez. Thanks,"

"Jesus, it's hot today," Harris said when we hit the trail. "You think anyone would mind if I took a swim?" he asked me.

"As long as there are two adults or a lifeguard on the dock," I teased. Luanne would have no problem disciplining him if he broke the rules. "Under the circumstances, Luanne might wave your day fees," I smiled.

"She takes her job very seriously."

"She feels like this is somehow her fault. This is Luanne's kingdom. When things are good, she can sit in her chair and knit. When things are bad, she works hard to fix them. She can't fix this one, and it's tough on her," I explained.

We were at the spot where the murder occurred. Harris stopped and looked out at the dock. There was yellow crime scene tape tied to the trees blocking both ramps. "You heard anything interesting today?" he asked without looking at me.

"Only that Emily will not be missed. Pretty much everyone hated her."

"Hate is a strong word," Harris said, reminding me of my dad, who used to say that too.

I felt bad for saying it. "You're right. Poor Emily." I thought for a moment and then ask, "Do you know Tom Johnson?"

"I know Tom. Why?"

I told him the story about the sound system, and he laughed. I also explained how Tom had been out in the water last night and that Emily hadn't been welcome at Johnson Camp any longer, then how Tom had just assumed Emily had been murdered when we spoke to him this morning. I felt sad because I liked Tom.

"Maybe she had something on him?" I suggested. "Being self-proclaimed Guardian of Secrets and all."

"Maybe they were lovers," he said.

I laughed involuntarily. "Doubtful. I imagine she got her heart broken fifty years ago and held it against all of humanity until last night."

The thumping base of rap music let us know we were close to Randy's cabin far before we could see it. Harris knocked and opened the door without waiting for a response. Jacob Foster almost jumped out of his underwear when he saw us. He'd been enjoying a bowl of cereal on a folded up futon. His hair was stuck in a Mohawk shape from sleep. The shock of our entry made him spill milk onto his black boxer briefs and the sofa too.

"Jesus Christ! Don't you knock?"

I couldn't imagine either one of my boys saying that to two adults. My urge to discipline him was strong, but I let Harris handle it.

"We did knock, Jacob," Harris said unapologetically. "I'm Detective Harris. There's been an incident in camp. Now clean yourself up and come with me."

"What are you talking about? I didn't do anything. Where's my dad?"

"He's up at the pavilion. I guess you haven't heard there was a murder here this morning?" Harris said as he walked further into the room.

Jacob Foster was either a very good actor, or this was the first he'd heard of the murder. He shut his sassy mouth and opened his eyes wide. He'd looked like such a young man when I'd seen him yesterday, but now his vulnerability reminded me that he was just a year older than my oldest—still a kid.

Harris looked around the room casually as he spoke. He looked out the window toward the lake. The cabin was perched high on the peninsula with the entire front section on stilts. Through the trees was the entire lake, sprawled out like a glittering gemstone. To the left was Johnson Camp, the beach clearly visible. Below were the aluminum docks, conspicuously unobstructed.

I knew the view by heart since it was a rental cabin like mine. There were only three of these cabins in camp. The rest were leased to members. We always rented Birch because of its proximity to the water and the boat docks. Randy usually took Cedar. We've rented it before. I found the cabin to be dark, and I didn't like climbing down the hill to my boat. The third rental cabin was Chestnut. That was the cabin Emily had been renting. Birch and Cedar sell out in April of each year and some weeks actually go into a lottery. If you couldn't get your weeks, you may get stuck with Chestnut, which was a nice cabin with a beautiful view of the other side of the peninsula where the lake formed a cove. It would have been perfect if it weren't for the proximity to the outhouses. This was how Emily, being new to camp, would have gotten a cabin.

"Feeling better? You slept an awfully long time today."

Jacob stared at the officer as if wondering when that had become a lawful offense.

"What did you do last night?"

"What is there to do here? Nothing."

Were my kids going to say the same some day? In the past, their days were filled with long paddles, swimming, hikes, and as soon as it was dark, they hit the paths with games of Manhunt. They often came home when we were already in bed, knees scraped from tripping over things in the dark, filthy and tired. But there were no other young people here yet, no late-night games, nothing but a small group of quiet adults. I suddenly felt very sorry for Jacob Foster.

I watched Harris look around the cabin. The knotty pine walls seemed darker than my cabin, more chestnut than honey colored. The tiny galley kitchen had dark cabinets too. There was a mounted bass over the futon, and a couple of wooden paddles were used as curtain rods. I'd always wanted to paint the cabinets and brighten the place up.

"Get dressed, Jake. We'll wait outside."

Harris and I moved out to the porch. I looked the detective in the eyes to see if I could figure out what he was thinking. "You don't think—?" I whispered.

"It's not like he was up on his computer all night. And why didn't his father bring him this morning?" Harris spoke casually, almost like he was whistling.

"I might have let me kids sleep in too. I mean, who wants to wake a kid up and tell them someone was murdered?" I said.

"Until two thirty in the afternoon? I never let my kids sleep that late," he said.

"Who died?" Jacob asked, coming out to meet us.

CHAPTER 15

Twilight fell upon the lake, and the glowing amber lights came on, one by one, in the cabins nestled into the hillside. From the water, the camp looked like a medieval village. Fires roared and campers walked past windows, cleaning up after dinner, shuffling cards or opening their books. Across the lake, prayers were said quietly, and pious ladies continued to show up for exercises in salvation without the bullhorn demands of the puffy little evangelist. On the lake, a lonely fisherman basked in solitude, and two beavers continued their work of genius, hauling branches from near and far.

I sat in the dark on my patio, looking down at the dock, imagining what had happened last night. *Was it before our night swim? Did I go to bed while Emily bled out on the dock just a hundred yards away? Or did some sinister event take place while I slept? Did a murderer walk right past my cabin in the dark? Who in camp would do such a thing?*

I heard footsteps approaching, and I sat perfectly still as they went to the door of the cabin behind me. My heart stopped a little, until I heard a knock.

"Ms...Lee?" It was Detective Harris, and demanding that he call me by my first name was turning out to be quite a punishment for him.

"I'm out here," I said loud enough for him to locate me.

He came down the path to the small patio.

"Still here?" I asked.

"Yes, still here. Carter and I are going to be camping with you all tonight, just until forensics finishes up tomorrow." He was wearing jeans and a polo shirt.

"Nice. Isn't Mrs. Harris going to miss you?"

"No. Mrs. Harris died five years ago next month. Cancer." He looked down at the ground, as if looking me in the eye would hurt too much.

"I'm so sorry," I said, knowing that wouldn't help. "Bourbon?" I lifted my glass. It always helped me.

"Wish I could, but I'm on the job."

"Well, at least have a seat. Please."

He sat next to me, sharing my view. It was normally quite beautiful, but that night the only thing before me was the dock.

"I wake up here, make my coffee, and then head there to do yoga. I read, contemplate life, take my boat out and bring it back to that dock. My kids fish off of it. We have camp friends over and watch for shooting stars from its deck," I said. "The beavers swim by every morning and every evening at around seven. If you aren't looking for them, they will pass you silently without notice. A couple of times we've surprised each other. It's my quiet place."

We sat in silence for a few moments.

"It looks like it was an accident. I don't know if that is going to help you feel better about being here," he said.

"What? Really?" This was good news. I started to think about what I had seen. "What do you think happened?"

"Well, we found hair and blood on the boat racks there." He pointed toward the dock. "According to the medical examiner, she was pushed with quite some force—nothing a simple fall could do. But I'll bet you five bucks whoever did it didn't mean to kill her."

"So you think someone just got mad and pushed her? Everyone was mad at her. But what was she doing down there at night? It doesn't make sense."

No one went down to that dock at night. Even during the day it was unusual to see many people. The swim docks were where the general public went.

"I just can't imagine what she was doing down there in her robe at night," I thought out loud. "And whose shoe prints were those? Somebody was there."

"Shoe prints? We only found your little mishap and Luanne's foot prints."

"Luanne didn't leave any footprints. She came onto the dock from the opposite side. She always comes that way." I pointed to the left side of the dock. "She came and left from there. The prints were on the right. Plus, Luanne has no use for flip-flops. She always wears sneakers. Those were flip-flop prints." I dug into my pocket and pulled out my phone. "Look. See what I mean?"

The officer frowned and shook his head.

"Damn! We thought you guys had made those."

"Well, they could be the killer's—or should I say the pusher's—shoes."

"No question about it, they killed her. People do foolish things when they are scared or mad. My question is, why on earth would anyone want to kill Emily English?" he asked. "I mean, what's the motive?"

"I think that you also have to take the cabin lottery into consideration."

"Tell me some more about that, please."

"Of Montego's sixteen cabins, three are rentals: mine, Emily's, and Randy Foster's. The rest have five-year leases. Some of them have been occupied for generations. Like the one over there." I pointed to the Rices' cabin. The porch light was on, but the cabin itself was dark. "And that one." I pointed to Roz and Moe's. "A few are less desirable because they're way up on the hill. But these...we're talking about waterfront property only thirty miles away from New York City. I doubt anyone would kill over a one hundred year old shack without indoor plumbing, but one never knows.

"The Rice family has always had that cabin. They feel they own it at this point. See the path?" I pointed to the spot that ran along my place and down to the dock. "That path used to go from there to the road and lead down to the dock. Marge Rice didn't like people walking past her cabin, so they covered up the path and planted on it. They've remodeled that entire place over the years and aren't planning on giving it up anytime soon. But their lease is up, and they don't do a thing around here. Marge serves on the board of directors, but that's only one meeting once a month. Talk to Lu about what goes on in those meetings. It's rigged so that the older families never lose their places."

"You don't seem too fond of the Rices," Harris said.

"Marge Rice is always nice to my face. But she is toxic. I've caught her complaining about Lu down at the swim docks in front of everyone. She wants to replace Lu with her nineteen-year-old niece. Camp would go to shit without Luanne. She is the glue that keeps this place together. There are a lot of politics here. That's why my family doesn't have a lease even though we've been coming here for eight years. We stay out of it."

"Toxic enough to commit murder?" he asked me.

"We're all capable of murder, Detective."

The lake had calmed to evening glass. Across the water, flames from a large bonfire could be seen on Johnson Beach. We sat in silence as it burned.

"*THEY WOULDN'T BE SECRETS IF I told you what they were, now would they?*" Emily's last words were burning in my brain. Something about that moment just didn't seem right. Why would she say something like that to a complete stranger?

The cabin was black with night. Sleep was not coming my way anytime soon, as every crunch of a leaf, every groan of the trees, filled me with fear. I was lying on my bed, trying not to think about Emily when I finally dozed off. The crackle of footsteps on the path woke me again. I wasn't sure how long I had been asleep, but it felt like just moments. The sound was headed toward the dock...no, it stopped at my cabin! I jumped out of bed, grabbed a paddle, and stood perfectly still behind the bedroom door. The doorknob jiggled a bit. I could feel the adrenaline racing through my veins, but instead of feeling strong, I felt weak and shaky. I wondered if I had the strength to hit the intruder hard enough and then thought about screaming. The door was bolted, but literally every half-wall-sized window in the cabin was open. It would just take a knife to open up the screen and climb in. Who would try the door?

"Lee!" I heard a whisper and then a slight rap on the glass pane of the door. "Lee! Honey!" There was another rap.

I switched the porch light on and stood there in my tank top and underpants, paddle in hand, ready to swing. It was my husband Jack.

I opened the door.

"What the fuck? What are you doing here? What happened to you?"

Obviously he'd taken a fall, because he had blood and dirt on his arm and knees. His face had a scratch like he'd walked into a thorn bush. And he was a sweaty mess. I stood aside so he could come in and turned the inside light on.

"I walked here from the highway. In the dark! I tried to get into camp this evening, and the little douche bag at the gate wouldn't let me in, so I parked on the highway and trekked in."

"Did you have a flashlight?" I asked.

"I didn't want to use it. I was worried they would see me."

"You are so lucky you didn't run into a bear! Oh my god! You scared me to death."

He grabbed me and held me in his arms, then let go and held my face in his hands.

"I didn't want you sleeping here alone tonight. If anything happened to you..." His eyes welled up.

"Let me look at you. Sit down." It was confusing. This was the man I was thinking about leaving. Now here he was, acting as protector. I was both annoyed and honored at the same time.

I poured some water into a bowl and got a wet towel to clean him up. "You walked all that way in the dark? You're crazy," I said, checking his hair and neck for ticks like he was one of my kids.

He swatted me away. "I'm fine. Give me that." He took the towel and cleaned his arm and knees. It wasn't as bad as it looked. "I tripped over a tree root." He laughed a little, showing me that his testy behavior was momentary.

I spent the rest of the evening catching him up on the events of the last three days.

"So, who did it?" he asked.

"I don't know! Do I look like Poirot? I only know who didn't do it: me. Otherwise, it could be anyone."

"But the shoes, they were small you said? So it had to be a woman, right?" he asked.

"Not necessarily. Someone could've just wanted it to look that way."

We got into the bed we had shared for so many years without saying a word about our own troubles. As he snuggled up against me, I thought of moving away. But he was rubbing his fingers along my shoulder and down my arm, and I forgot all about our differences, remembering only the beautiful familiarity and comfort of our long partnership. My mind wandered through the events of the day, but exhaustion prevented me from finding any answers to Emily's murder. From across the lake, I heard the sound of thunder. A concert of heavy raindrops falling on the roof and the ground around me lulled me to sleep.

CHAPTER 17

"Is it selfish of me to want them to get out of here so I can get to my boat?" Red was still siting in the water, witness to the deadly event. "I came here to paddle."

"I thought you came here to get away from me," Jack said, handing me a cup of hot coffee while I was still in bed.

The heavy rain that washed through camp was gone, and the sun took its place among a pastel sky.

"Can we not talk about that now? This trip away was supposed to be time for me to get some things straight in my head, and now you're here."

"I'm not making demands on you, Lee. Honestly. I was worried about your safety. I'll give you all the space you need."

When I thought of what he went through to get to me I felt bad. With all that had happened in the past few days, I was having a hard time remembering why I was so mad at him in the first place. "Sorry. I know why you came, and I appreciate it. Thanks to you, I slept like a baby last night. Before you got here I was imagining a ratty-robed woman with wild white hair haunting the docks. I had the blankets over my head."

His laugh brought relief from the tension between us.

"I have to go tell Detective Harris you're here. Just stay put until I come back for you, okay?"

When I stepped out of the cabin a little while later, Roz was coming back from her morning paddle. She was carrying her solo canoe, the love of her life and the envy of mine. The little boat weighed only twenty-six pounds. She had made it herself in the basement of her Staten Island home.

Roz was up every day at the crack of dawn for a paddle and was sure to be seen there again at sunset. If you asked her how it went, you would hear magical tales from the natural world. Maybe she'd found a bird's nest on a branch that dangled over the water or two turtles mating on a rock. She knew all the birdcalls from experience, and if you wanted to know where the blueberries were ripe, she'd send you in the right direction.

Roz was a robust woman, with a thick Staten Island accent and an even thicker skin. She never talked badly about anyone, but if she had an issue, she wasn't shy about telling you. The woman loved to cook and fed most everyone in camp several times per summer.

I felt envious as she hung her boat on the rack on the side of her cabin. If Harris didn't open the dock soon, I would need to borrow a club boat, and the fleet was mostly made up of heavy plastic scuppers.

"What have you got there?" I asked. She had pulled a bundle of sticks from the boat before hanging the canoe on the wall, where its forest green bottom matched perfectly with her freshly painted picnic table and the trim around her doors and windows. It was against park rules to paint anything without permission, but she'd been doing it for so long that no one could remember it any other way.

"I found a fallen birch. I was able to pull up next to it and break these off. They might make good arrows if they're whittled. I figured it would give Jacob something to do. The poor kid's bored to death," she said, feeling the many pockets on her fishing vest as if searching for something specific.

She stood staring at me a moment, and I felt self-conscious. I was not looking my best. "Come here," she insisted.

I walked over to her patio and sat on one of the benches.

"No, no. Here." She led me to her hammock. "Get in," she ordered.

I obeyed, and once in, I felt weightless in both mind and body.

"Here you go." She handed me a stick and a pocketknife. "You look like you could use a whittle." She laughed a little at her own statement and then sat next to me in a plastic chair. We both worked on sharpening the edges of a stick, first removing the white bark carefully then working on the tip. After several swipes of the knife, I put the stick down and looked up past the treetops to the sky.

"You are such a good cruise director, Roz," I said in a dreamy, "the sky is beautiful" kind of voice.

"You looked like you could use a break, honey."

"Jack snuck into camp late last night. Nearly scared the daylights out of me."

She nodded. "I heard him. I was happy I didn't have to come out with my bear spray."

I laughed, thinking of my own defensive posture before I'd know who it was at the door.

"You'd better tell that Sheriff before he gets his panties in a knot," she warned me.

"Yeah, that's where I was headed." We whittled some more before I asked, "Hey, Roz, you guys didn't hear a thing the other night? When Emily was killed?"

She shook her head no, but didn't look at me. Instead she focused on her stick. "That woman was trouble from the moment she drove through the gate. Her snooping and clawing for a place here, pushing herself on us like we had to take what she was selling." Roz shook her head as if she were disappointed. "Shame on her. Shame."

"I guess I missed a lot this summer," I said.

"If by missed, you mean avoided that complaining troublemaker, you didn't miss a thing. She's been walking around here like we're a bunch of misfits, griping about the paths not being cleared, the bathrooms having spiders, the beds not being comfortable. You're in the forest, lady. Why don't you go back to your rent-controlled apartment and complain about your cheap rent? I had a tenant like her once. I kicked her out after three months."

Roz was an old-school conservative, fiscally anyway. She didn't care what you did with your personal life so long as she didn't have to pay for it. I avoided politics at all costs because I found that many of my camp friends were far more to the right than I was.

"She felt like she was entitled to everything. It doesn't surprise me at all that she was killed. What really surprises me is that someone didn't do it sooner. She's been up here for four weeks now, and guess what? Not one visitor. Can you imagine? All this and no one to share it with." Her voice softened a bit as she looked around the woods, her eyes resting on the lake. "Then she tells me she wants to be on the cabin committee. Okay. Sure." She shrugged. "Starts bossing me around, going into the rental cabins and complaining that they aren't clean. Is your cabin clean?"

"It's always clean, Roz," I assured her. "Spotless."

"She was a pain in the ass," she mumbled. "I love the people in this camp. Every last one of them." She was quiet for a second and then added, "I didn't hear a thing."

I lay back in the hammock with my sharp stick in hand, playing with the tip while I watched loose white clouds drift by the tiny opening in the treetops. I was grateful for the breeze that rustled the leaves and grateful for that moment beside my dear friend, who wanted to share her hammock and little pieces of happiness with me. Quiet, perfect little bits of heaven. Lying there so carefree for a few moments, I felt like I could live forever.

"Well, listen, hon," Roz finally said. "We're goin' over to West Point to hear some classical music on the lawn. Stay as long as you want. I mean it; stay put." Then she left me in the hammock to wonder whom she was protecting.

CHAPTER 18

JED HARRIS WAS LEAVING EMILY'S cabin, pulling rubber gloves off of his hands as I arrived. "Nothing. Not here or in the car." He shook his head. "Forensics will be here soon. Unfortunately, anything down on the dock is now part of the lake thanks to the rain."

I thought of Emily's blood in the water, and it made my stomach turn. "Ugh," I said involuntarily. I wondered why they didn't tent the site but didn't want to ask in case the question embarrassed him.

"Squeamish for a sleuth," he joked.

"I'm a vegetarian. I won't be putting my face in the lake for a while. Hey! Does that mean I can go get my boat? I need a paddle more than I can tell you," I pleaded.

"Is that what you came to ask me?"

"No, actually I came to tell you something—a few things really. For starters, my husband, Jack, hiked into camp last night. He's in my cabin."

I wasn't really sure what Harris would say, but he just said, "Okay then."

"He was really worried about my safety," I added.

"What else?"

"Do you have time of death yet?"

"That's a question." He was cranky. Maybe he hadn't slept well in the great room last night. I was going to tell him about Bobby going into the cabin, but I couldn't. Not before I spoke to Bobby about it.

"Do you?" I asked again with my most appealing smile.

"The pathologist says she was alive for a while. Time of death was sometime in early dawn. The head wound happened between 9 and 10 p.m."

"That's just awful. Do you mean that, if we had found her sooner, we could have saved her?"

"She was alive, but that just means her organs were working. Medical Examiner says she was doomed after the blow. The fall back fractured her skull. Lots of swelling and bleeding." He mimicked her fall, standing on one foot and pretending to fall backward. I had to try not to laugh and must have looked very strange as I stood there smiling. "Then the force of the blow sent her flying forward, and she cracked her temple on the dock when she landed. Toast." He shifted his feet and pretended to fall forward. I almost lost it, and he smiled back at me. "You like that, do you?" he laughed.

I felt like I had permission to let out a little giggle, and it was a release. I've been known to lose it when I hold my laughter in. I can look like a hysterical lunatic. "We all had dinner that night on Roz and Moe's patio. It had to happen later, after we went to the swim docks. Otherwise we would have heard or seen something. So it couldn't have been any of us."

"But you weren't together all evening were you? Roz says you guys left in the boat at a quarter past nine. Her clock said nine twenty-five when she got back from the docks," he told me.

"When we came back, it was probably ten. That gets everyone who was on the boat off the hook...Randy and Delia, Maddy and Henry, and myself. But I would have been able to hear anyone going down to the dock from my cabin. So I would say it had either already happened before ten, or much later. I was asleep by eleven. I know that for sure because I looked at my phone before I went to bed."

I really couldn't imagine anyone at the lake doing this. But some-one did.

I went back to my cabin to get Jack. Bobby adored my husband. I'd be more likely to get the truth out of him with Jack by my side.

Bobby's cabin was one of the most remote on the peninsula. To get there, you had to follow the footpath from our cabin to the road. Then you had to cross down behind the outhouses and follow the winding path to the other side of the peninsula. The cabins on that side of camp were like a different district from ours; the views were different, the cabins were further apart, and they faced the east cove, the one that had the large rock at the end of it.

We knocked on Bobby's door. It was only 9:30 a.m., so I was surprised when he answered, fully dressed, with a somewhat clean shirt on.

"Look what I found," I said, and then stepped aside so he could see my husband standing there with a reluctant grin. Jack was an-noyed that I'd made him come with me, saying he wanted nothing to do with the whole mess and protesting that we shouldn't get involved. He was concerned about my safety.

"Jack! My man!" Bobby shook Jack's hand warmly. "I'd invite you in, but it's kind of a mess in here right now." He stepped out in his bare feet.

"No sweat," Jack replied. "I just wanted to say hello."

"Are you staying?"

I didn't know the answer to that question myself. I looked at my husband.

"Well, I'm not leaving my wife when there is a murderer on the loose."

"Yeah, pretty weird stuff, huh?" He scratched his head as if it would help. "Here, sit down."

We took a seat at his picnic table, which leaned down the hill a little precariously. I was glad he was sitting on the topside of the hill; it anchored the table. His view of the lake was spectacularly clear and private.

"What do you think happened?" I asked him.

"Hell if I know," he said, shaking his head.

"Bobby, what were you doing in Emily's cabin yesterday?" It was a blunt approach, but I couldn't see how tiptoeing around the question was going to get me any further. I'd known Bobby a long time and felt I could be direct.

"What? I told you yesterday. I was making sure the place was locked."

I looked at him, head tilted, waiting for the truth. "I didn't tell the cops I saw you there. Neither did Luanne as far as I know. Just tell me the truth. I mean, you wouldn't even take her door off because she wasn't there. It doesn't make any sense to me that you would go inside a dead woman's cabin."

"Lee, I..." He looked to Jack for help, but Jack shrugged in support.

"I don't think you killed her, Bobby. I just know something is up. I've never heard you call anyone a bitch. It's not like you. Why the intense dislike?"

He shook his head and exhaled deeply. "She was blackmailing me."

"Blackmailing you? What? How? This is summer camp for God's sake."

"She took a video of me working on the steps down to the swim dock. I was feeling good that day. I mixed and poured concrete. I paid for it that night—let me tell you—but that day I felt like I could do it. I saw her standing there, but I didn't look up to see what she was doing. Later, she showed me the clip on her phone. 'You don't look so disabled to me,' she said. I didn't think too much of it at the time, but the next day I ran into her and she said, 'You know, I'm in the lottery for a cabin.' I said, 'That's great, Emily.' What the hell did I care? Right? 'Well, I know you're on the Board, and you are going to help me get a cabin,' she tells me. 'What makes you think that?' I asked her. And she says, 'Because if I don't get a cabin, I am going to show my video to the Department of Health. I looked it up. They have a fraud hotline. You don't look disabled to me.'"

Bobby's head was low, his shoulders hunched in defeat. "I should have told her to go fuck herself!" he said. "But what difference does it make now?"

"So you were looking for her phone?" I asked

"Yeah, I was looking for her phone. I was going to try to delete the video."

"Did you find it?"

"No. I didn't really look. The cabin was upside down when I walked in. I just turned around and walked right back out."

"The forensics team is coming today, Bobby. Are they going to find your prints in there?" I asked.

"No. Really. I didn't touch a thing. After I saw that mess, I figured I wasn't the only one she was blackmailing."

"She was really something, that woman. She caught me swimming off the rock the other day and tattled to Luanne. Right in front of me!" I told him. "I guess it's better than getting blackmailed."

"Yeah, well Luanne knew all about her." He looked away, like he didn't want me to see something in his eyes.

"Are you trying to say that she had something on Luanne?"

"What do I know? I'm just sayin'," he said shrugging his shoulders and tightening his mouth with an East Coast, blue-collar tough guy kind of attitude. Luanne was the same way. Even though he and Luanne didn't like each other, neither would break the old-school Brooklyn pact by ratting each other out.

"So how are the wife and kids?" asked Jack, changing the subject. My husband knew how to talk to just about anyone, and I admired how he now genuinely listened to a story about one of Bobby's kids. In spite of the tough night, Jack's shirt was clean and his appearance neat. His thick dark hair looked as if he'd just left the mirror, and his jawline was darkened from a morning without a blade. He was quite handsome, and I found myself admiring him in a sex-starved kind of way.

He saw me watching him and looked me in the eyes with a smile. I felt a little flare of excitement, fresh and lusty. I smiled back then looked away.

"Well, I've got to hike out to my car. I left it on the highway last night," he told Bobby.

"Yeah, Randy and I are supposed to be working on some railings for the pavilion. It doesn't seem appropriate to me. I don't know. It feels like we should be more reverent." Bobby and Randy were dear old friends. They were often seen working on projects around camp.

"Something tells me Emily would have preferred the maintenance." I chuckled to myself as I got up.

"You coming?" Jack asked me, and I nodded to let him know I was.

I followed him down the trail that led past Bobby's cabin and out of camp toward the highway. It was a beautiful day, cool and dry: a good day to be on the water. There was no wind, and the lake had an after-rain clean to it. The hike was about a mile or so and followed the shoreline. We stopped at the big rock where I had met Emily just two days before. I told Jack the story while we watched the white puffy clouds reflect on the water, the sky so blue that the lake surface gazed back in perfect likeness.

The car was still there, only now it had a ticket flapping from the windshield. Jack drove a 6 series BMW. I hated the car. Every jackass on the road drove a BMW. Not that everyone who drove a BMW was a jackass. I was sure there were nice people who drove them. But if someone were tailing me in the fast lane—even when there was a car in front of me—it was usually a BMW. They were the first choice in car for the arrogant.

I looked in the backseat. Not even a crumb. Nothing was stuffed into the side-door pockets either. No sports equipment, handheld video games, or food wrappers. No hint of family. I thought about my own very unsexy car, with the food stains and the cleat-shaped mud patties, and felt bitter. Jack got a free pass on everything kid-related. We'd gotten in a huge fight when he first brought the car home. It was right after his annual bonus, which is enormous for the Wall Street guys. We'd always had a rule that no matter how much money we had, we wouldn't spend it on new cars. (Okay, it was my rule, but I didn't make many and this was important to me.) When I saw how much this car had cost, I flipped out.

"It's embarrassing and ostentatious and it's just wrong!" I'd yelled.

"I think it is cooool!" Max had roared, which had made me even angrier.

"Great. Teach your children well, Jack."

"I work hard, Lee. I should be able to buy myself a toy once in a while. Just drive it. It's amazing," he'd pleaded.

"I will never step foot in that car," I swore. Of course I'd had to break that vow and get in it once in a while, and I'd been known to drive it. It handled like a dream. But it didn't make me like it any more.

It took some doing to get back into camp. I explained to the officer on duty that Jack was my husband and that Detective Harris already knew he was there. Finally, he radioed the detective, and we were allowed to pass.

"Park in the first lot," I told Jack. I didn't want my friends to see the car. I was embarrassed by our wealth. My parents had both been college professors. My mother had written a much-used philosophy textbook, and my father a couple of well-received novels. But they were very bohemian, and if you came to our home, which was in a very good part of San Francisco, most people would have thought they were struggling. Our furniture was worn, and there was unframed art crowding the walls and stacked up in corners. They had one car, and it was an old beat up station wagon. My parents were green before green was in. They didn't believe in consumerism and practiced using what they had until they couldn't anymore.

Both of them were incredibly generous people. Our family spent two Saturdays a month working in St. Anthony's kitchen, serving food to the many homeless in San Francisco. Family vacations usually included some kind of volunteer work, and we always came back with empty suitcases, leaving behind our clothing for those who needed it most.

My sisters and I had a substantial trust account left for us. I was grateful to be a comfortable orphan instead of a poor one. My parents had put together a financial plan when my father got sick. Although they had left us plenty, they still donated about half of their estate to the charities that they loved. We never resented this because we knew the organizations and were of like mind.

Jack's parents were upper crust Connecticut. His father made his fortune the same way Jack did, and his grandfather held some important patents. They were low key about their spending too, but in an old money way. The house on Nantucket was only remodeled when they inherited it...that kind of money.

"I need your help with something. No judgment. Just help," I told him on the way into camp.

"No judgment?" he shook his head, completely ignoring my request. "I had no choice, Lee. My car was my only way up here. You had the other car."

"I know, I know. I'm sorry. I can't help it. It's embarrassing—Luanne and Maddy struggle. I don't want to show up to camp in an automobile that costs more than they make in a year.

"I need your help. For real," I repeated.

"You want me to hide the murder weapon?"

"Very funny. I'm a thief, not a murderer."

If he'd been on the swim dock that evening, he would have been furious with me. He's very proper and does not celebrate April Fool's Day as though it were a national holiday like I do. And since he never gets drunk, he doesn't wake up the next day wishing something hadn't occurred. He leaves that all to me.

When I told him that we had stolen the PA system from Johnson Camp, the disappointment was all over his face.

"No judgment!" I reminded him.

"I didn't say a word. So how are you planning on dragging me into this?" he asked.

"I need to talk to Tom, and I need to return the PA system, so you are going to help me get it out of the war canoe and into Red without me dunking it in the lake." I thought a minute. "Or maybe I should give it a quick dunk before I return it..."

He gave me another disapproving look.

"Oh, just wait until that woman gets her PA back. You'll be paddling over there yourself to shut her up," I said. "I wish someone would put her down," I mumbled, not meaning it and feeling awful right after it came out.

As we walked back to camp, Jack put his arm around my shoulder and pulled me in. I resisted, and he pulled me in harder, so I punched him in his firm stomach, and he grabbed me and pulled me in close with both arms. I felt like a weak little child. I looked up at him and was lost for a moment, forgetting our problems and Emily and feeling a little lusty toward him.

"Get a room!" a voice shouted from up the road. It was Luanne. She and Maddy were on their way out the camp road for their morning walk. They greeted Jack with the same genuine warmth they'd given me when I arrived.

"You're lucky they didn't shoot you," Luanne said about his hike in last night.

"He's lucky he didn't run into a bear," I repeated.

"Hey, we're headed over to Johnson Camp to return the PA," I told them.

"Oh God, please. I get agita every time I think about it," Luanne said.

"What are you worried about? Tommy doesn't even care. He's as happy as we are to shut that woman up," Maddy reminded her.

"Please. It's not right," she said, shaking her head. Poor Luanne. Her life had been one long succession of doing the right thing. She married her husband because she was pregnant. She had three more because birth control was a sin. She stayed with him because the church told her she had to. I wished I could just free her from her self-inflicted compliance. It was wonderful how she never held those around her up to the same standards. If only she would give herself the same break.

"We'll get it back, Luanne. No worries," I assured her.

CHAPTER 19

WHATEVER MOMENT JACK AND I had together in camp was over once we hit the water. I was in my canoe with the PA system wrapped in a towel and stuffed into a large beach bag, paddling across the lake with a view of Jack's back, which was getting smaller and smaller by the moment. He arrived on the Johnson Beach before I had even hit the halfway mark. Instead of being upset at his leaving me behind, I decided to take my time and try to enjoy the paddle I had been longing for since yesterday morning. Jack stood on the shore waiting for me, and I tried to convince myself not to be angry with him. *So we will never paddle quietly through the water together. So what? I like paddling alone,* I reminded myself.

The beach was deserted, and I had the opportunity to really see it. There was very little sand, which surprised me because, in the past, the Johnsons had taken great pride in being the only sandy beach on the lake. Plastic bottles were strewn about. A single barrel was overflowing with trash. I almost stepped on a rusty can in the water and held it up.

"Jesus," Jack whispered.

He took the beach bag from me and threw it over his shoulder, and we hiked up the steep hill to Tom's office. The once paved path was filled with ruts, and you could kick the asphalt loose if you tried.

I hadn't been to the Johnson Camp in the daylight for a long time. Jack looked at me, and we both raised our eyebrows. There was a time when this was quite a charming place. The hill at Johnson Camp was very steep, and the cabins were somewhat close together. The little chestnut structures still had their original bark and were as sweet as ever on their own, but there were missing railings and chipped paint on the forest green doors. A fallen tree had been left where it landed, some piles of wood laid where someone had attempted and then abandoned clean up. It took a lot of maintenance to keep these old camps looking good. We were lucky to have Bobby and so many of the other volunteers in camp. Without them, Montego could look the same.

As we got closer to the office, nervousness was replaced by embarrassment. I felt like I was being walked back to school by a parent after being suspended. Jack got to the door before me.

"Wait!" I said. "Don't go in without me. This is my doing."

He held the door open for me and used one arm to usher me in. The office looked exactly as it would have in 1927, when it was built. A wooden counter separated Tom's office from what would be the waiting area. There were cubbies with keys and notes inside some of the boxes.

No one was in the office, however, so we headed toward the A-framed dining hall, where I could hear the clanging of silverware and female chatter. The dining hall had been built in the early sixties, and it looked exactly like it had on opening day. Large round tables were half-filled with ladies laughing, eating, and sharing stories. A buffet of processed food items and plastic-wrapped condiments were spread across the back wall.

We also found Tom arguing with everyone's favorite evangelical bully. She was wearing a white-hooded beach cover-up, too short to hide her dimpled round thighs. Her thin hair was in a high ponytail, half of which had fallen around her neck. She looked like a tiny terrier barking at a large Labrador retriever. Two of her supporters stood behind her, nodding in agreement whenever she finished a sentence.

Tom spotted us but could not get out of the conversation. He nodded for us to go through the kitchen door, where a couple of local teens were slicing bagels on a large stainless steel table.

"This is for you," I said, handing Tom the bag as he walked in the door.

He looked at the bag without taking it.

"Is that what I think it is?"

"Yes, it is."

"Well, I don't really want that," he said, not calling it by name so his workers wouldn't know.

"Really?" I smiled. "Well, what shall I do with it?"

"Throw it in the lake for all I care," he said.

"Why would I do a thing like that to such a nice lake?" I asked him.

"We'll just leave it in the office, and you can do what you'd like with it," Jack said with authority. I knew him so well. He was thinking that if we returned it, I'd be off the hook legally.

Tom sighed. "What's the word on Emily? Do they have a suspect yet?"

"I don't know. I've been wanting to ask you though—why did she leave Johnsons?"

"That woman was the biggest pain in my ass. I tried to be nice to her. I did. My wife tried too. She made our lives hell with her complaints. She threatened to call Parks on me if I didn't replace her mattress because it was too hard on her back. She made me drive her down to the beach on the golf cart because she was 'disabled,' yet she hiked all over this goddamned lake every day she was here. Disabled my ass. And she tortured these guys over every meal."

The two kids looked up at the mention of them and nodded in agreement.

"That old lady was nuts," the young girl said.

"Crazy like a fox," I said.

"What do you mean?" Tom asked.

I didn't want to tell him about Bobby. "Let's just say she was in the habit of collecting information," I said.

"I don't know anything about that," he said. "Our good fortune was your bad luck. Her discovering Montego was the best thing that's happened to me in a long time."

"Well, you sure have a full house now," I laughed.

He rolled his eyes.

"Be careful what you wish for, right? It gets harder and harder to keep this place each year. After this fiasco, I may just hand the property back over to Parks."

I was frankly surprised the park system hadn't taken it back already. It was obvious that maintenance had gotten away from the Johnson family. These were hundred-year-old cabins and grounds. It was always going to be something. You couldn't make alterations to a building without their permission because of their historic nature, but the leaseholder was required to make all approved repairs.

Tom looked tired and much older than his years. His blond hair was thin and mixed with gray. The lines on his face spelled disappointment.

Jack stood with his hands deep in his pockets. He didn't have anything to say that would help the poor man, so he just stayed quiet.

"I can't imagine a Johnson Camp without a Johnson," I said. "But life is short. Go do something that makes you happy."

"Yeah, tell my wife that," he said.

"Hey, Tom, I've been meaning to ask you something." I waited for his permission to continue.

"Yeah, what?" he asked.

"Where were you coming from that night we saw you on the beach?"

"I was retrieving a canoe. Someone didn't tie it up properly, and it drifted," he answered with a slightly annoyed tone.

"Did it drift all the way to Montego?"

"I didn't kill Emily if that's what you're getting at! Jesus Christ, what are you the police?" he snarled. Big soft Tom had had enough.

The two teenagers looked up from their bagels with wide eyes.

"Sorry! I just wondered if you saw anything. I'm not accusing you, Tom," I played defensive.

"Let's go, hon," Jack said. "You take care, Tom," he called out as we left.

We walked toward the office without speaking.

"Jeesh," I whispered when we got inside.

"You basically accused him of murder. What did you expect?"

"He was on the water that night, Jack, and he was acting very oddly when he saw us."

"Maybe he was surprised to see a drunken band of thieves on his beach?"

"It was more than that," I said as I walked behind the counter to drop the beach bag off somewhere inconspicuous.

I moved slowly, so that I had time to look around his desk. It was neat, like his kitchen. There was a stack of delivery invoices and a notepad with a few messages written in round, girlish writing.

"Come on, Lee. Let's go," Jack demanded like I was one of our boys.

There were three messages:

Call Joan
Steve Hendrix called; he needs a payment on the produce
T called again.

"Who's T?" I said out loud.

"Come on! Tom is coming!" Jack said through clenched teeth, as if Tom could read his lips.

We left the office, and as we headed down the path, Tom approached us again. "Look, I'm sorry I snapped. You can't believe the pressure I'm under here. If these ladies weren't leaving on Friday, there would probably be another murder on this lake. And they would have a hard time figuring out if it was my wife, the staff, or me. We're all tired of taking that woman's abuse. The irony is, I booked them so I wouldn't have to deal with people like Emily. If she called for a cabin, I could say we were full and mean it."

Tom was so defeated. It was terribly sad to see. I thought about the first time I had met him, eight years ago. He was the tan blond hottie on the lake. Luanne and Maddy told me to make sure I paddled over to get a look at him, so from my boat I'd waved and he'd waved back from the lifeguard stand. They were right. Tom had been the treat from Johnson Camp. He'd still had joy back then, and joy is so attractive. The recession had taken a real toll on people, and Tom Johnson was one of its casualties.

"Don't apologize, Tom. I'm the one who should be apologizing. I piled more onto your plate with our little gag. I'm terribly sorry."

He laughed. "It's actually made things a little better not to have that woman's voice any louder than it already is. If she represents Christianity, it's time for me to change religions." He shook his head, and when he smiled, I saw the old Tom. The handsome Tom. But it faded as fast as his expression. "You take care," he said to us as we headed down the steep narrow path.

"He's falling apart with the place," Jack said sadly.

I told Jack that I'd needed some time alone, and he raced off across the lake in relief. I stuck to the shallow edges and tried to find my perfect peace, but each time my mind cleared, another thought of Emily's murder pushed back in.

A fallen tree made its way into the lake. I could see its thin branches reaching down into the silt of the halcyon water. A couple of turtles were sunning on the trunk and slid into the deep on my approach.

What was Tom doing on the lake that night? The currents carried his boats straight to our docks, so if he was retrieving a boat, he may have seen Emily and maybe her murderer. Why wouldn't he just say so? Unless he was the one who had pushed her into that rack. But the footprints...none of it made sense to me. And why would Tom want to kill her? He was finally rid of her, unless she was blackmailing him too. And I'd only seen him with one boat that night. He was lying; I was sure of it.

A large splash startled me back to reality. At first I thought it was a beaver, but it was too late in the morning. I had alarmed an otter, and he was giving it back. I stayed cautiously still, filled with the joy of seeing the sleek creature dart below my boat. He came back up a few feet away, his silky head popping out of the water just enough to get a look at me.

The Otter was my son Max's favorite animal. Max loved the water so much when he was little that, by day's end, his eyes would be bloodshot and his fingers pruned. I didn't worry about applying sunblock because he was always a foot below the water, deep in exploration, his blond hair puffing about his head like a sea anemone, his little limbs grabbing and kicking like a tadpole. At noon, when I'd made him sit on the dock and eat, he would bite his sandwich and watch the water anxiously like it was about to dry up if he stayed out too long. I'd wrap him in a towel when he shivered, and then the sun would warm his shoulders, and it would be time to go back in.

The memory made me tear up. I longed for those days when he only wanted to be with me. If he were here, he'd be racing and darting about in his Kayak, sometimes spilling into the water to cool off. When his head bobbed up, his hair would be slicked back and silky like the otter's. But now a young man would rise, loud with laughter, and strong enough to pull himself onto his boat without my help.

"You're so slow, Mom," he would say and paddle off.

I sat there clouded with my aching memories until the otter reappeared on the other side of my boat, his little eyes full of sympathy for me. I used my paddle gently so as not to drift toward him, but that was enough to scare him away, and he disappeared for good.

CHAPTER 20

"IF YOU DON'T WANT HIM, let him know I'm available." Luanne was on the dock when I pulled in. She had a thermos of coffee in one hand and helped me up with the other. "I'm just sayin'. You could be married to my husband."

I felt a little ashamed. I'd been so busy whining about my life that I hadn't even asked Lu how things were going with her own unhappy marriage. "What's going on with you and Patrick?" I asked, tying Red to the dock.

"Ahhh, same ol' same ol'," she replied with brave resignation.

"I'm so sorry. I've been so wrapped up in my own drama. What's up?" I asked again.

We both looked at the dock. Normally, I left two canvas beach chairs here for my entire stay. I hadn't even had time to put them out yet when Emily's murder happened. Now I felt weird about sitting here.

"It's a little creepy down here," she said, reading my mind.

"No kidding. Should I get the chairs? Shit, I don't mean to be even more selfish, but this is my dock, you know?"

"I know. Maybe you have to find another spot?"

"No way," I said. "Wait here."

I walked up the hill and grabbed a beer and two canvas beach chairs from the side of my cabin. "We're going to have to move on," I said. "It'll get easier in time."

We sat on the opposite side of where it happened.

"So strange," she said, looking over to the spot where Emily died.

"I always thought someone would hit their head on those bars," I said.

"I've asked my husband to take them down five times now. I'm gonna get Henry and Jack to do it. No one even uses them anyway, and now they killed someone. I wonder if we're gonna get sued."

"According to Harris, Emily didn't have anyone in her life who would sue, Luanne. Don't worry about it," I said, knowing she would worry anyway. "Sad isn't it? To be so alone."

"Whatevah. That's what I'm sayin' now. Whatevah." She held up her hands like she was feeling for rain.

"Have you seen Jack?" I asked. His boat was on the shore, so I knew he'd come back.

"Last time I saw him he was drinking beer with Henry up at the pavilion."

He was keeping his promise to give me my space.

"So what's going on with Patrick, Luanne? And don't say 'nothing,'" I said when we were settled in our seats. I had my beer, and Luanne was still holding her plastic giveaway car mug of coffee, the logo long worn off.

"I think he's usin' again." Her eyes welled up, which I had only seen a handful of times, usually when someone from the board of directors hurt her feelings.

"Uh oh. What makes you think so?" I asked.

"He comes home from the bar short on tips. Even on a Friday night, when I know the bar is busy. Sometimes he claims the register was short and he had to throw in his tip money. Or he tells me it was slow. I just know after all these years. He's at it again."

"Oh shit, Luanne. What are you going to do?"

They had lost their home the last time he was doing drugs. It was before I knew them, but Luanne was still heartbroken over it. They'd spent her small inheritance on that house, the first they were ever able to own, and because of bad behavior it was gone.

Patrick was not my favorite guy. Luanne had told me too much, so by the time I had met him in person, the stories defined him. He was a small guy, barely making five foot six. His swollen belly didn't match the rest of his thin frame, thanks to a long habit of beer drinking. He was friendly, but what bugged me most about Patrick was his lack of humility. He knew all and was master of everything. And like most liars, he believed that we believed him. Since I'd know him, he'd told me he was once an electrician, accountant, and programmer. I shook my head in disappointment whenever I thought of him. Most people did.

"What can I do? Send him home to his mother? She won't take him anymore. I'm stuck with him. I gotta keep my money hidden just so I can pay the bills." She wiped a tear away as soon as it came out, like it would break her if it were able to make it down her cheek. "I can't afford to leave him. That's the thing. We're stuck together because of money. What little he's bringing home is needed so I can feed my girls and keep the lights on. I asked the Board for a raise last month. You'd think I was asking them for a million dollars. I haven't had a raise in three summers. You shoulda heard Marge telling me how there's no more money for salaries—that I'm the highest paid camp director they've evah had." She shook her head.

"As you should be," I responded. "This place would fall apart without you."

"No one's beating down the door to live up here every weekend from April to October. Full-time in the summer! Most people don't want to do that for the stipend they give me. I barely make enough to pay for gas and food. But I have the cabin, and according to Marge, that calls for gratitude."

"The cabin," I said. "Quite the commodity."

I looked out to the lake. The dense forest rolled toward an abrupt stop at the water line, threatening to jump in. Someone had taken out a white Sunfish with a rainbow sail, contrasting brightly under the enormous periwinkle sky.

"Did you see Tom over here on Tuesday night? He said he had to pick up a stray boat from our camp."

"Is that what they're callin' it now?" she laughed.

I turned away to face her. "What does that mean?"

She waved me away, "I gotta go. I'm gettin' a potluck together for dinner tonight. Can you make it?"

"You can't leave me hanging like that!" I pleaded.

"It's none of my business. I shouldn't have said anything. You comin' to the potluck or no?"

At first it sounded like a bad idea, but then I thought of sitting in the cabin with Jack, trying to explain to him how he was a kayak and I was canoe. He'd call me crazy, and then we would fight. "I'll be there," I promised.

As soon as she left, I pulled a joint out of my backpack and smoked the entire thing quickly, knowing police were nearby. I felt annoyed because it was supposed to be a habit of calm, and I was a responsible member of society. I rushed and hid like a criminal, which technically I was. If it had been a bottle of Xanax, no one would have had a problem with it. A doctor would have gotten his perks from prescribing a drug with adverse side effects including disinhibition, jaundice, hallucinations, constipation, and others, but it would be legal. Doctors don't get perks when people treat themselves with weed.

After finishing the joint, I left the chair and lay down onto the decking, stretching my limbs, then rising up again with an enormous exhale to join nature in her place of peace. I didn't think about the events of the day, or week, or year. Instead I absorbed the sun on my face and was grateful for my life. I felt joy, sunny warm joy. *I would live forever if I could feel like this every day.*

Solitude was elusive, and soon Therese was on her dock, stand up paddleboard in tow. With one athletic jump, she paddled away like a gondolier. She was following the line of the shore, and my dock was on the way. I shouted hello and told her Jack was in camp. The two of them were pals. She stopped briefly, but only long enough to ask after my boys. If it bothered her that I was doing yoga so close to a crime scene, she didn't let on.

"Did you know Emily?" I asked when Therese glanced at the surface of the dock.

"Yes, from lifeguarding at Johnson. She liked to swim. It was good for her joints." Her voice was as monotone as ever, so it was hard for me to measure how she felt about Emily.

She paddled on, her petite bronze frame gliding quietly on the glassy surface. *She is tiny. Tiny. Tiny feet.* I watched her round the bend as I continued my stretching. When she stopped at Johnson Camp, I made a decision and left my things on the dock in a hurry.

Therese's cabin was nestled in between Moe and Roz's and Delia and Randy's places, not quite close enough for a shout out. A weatherworn sign, rustic in design and painted with the word "Harriman" was tacked to the wall next to the door. The cabins were named when they were built, and this was the only original plaque that had survived. It had been handmade by people who had used the word gay to describe happy and called their partners "dear" and "darling." Back when all men were expected to be handy and women knew how to make a cake from scratch.

Therese always kept her shoes outside. I thought it was weird because spiders could crawl in there, but apparently that wasn't a concern for her. Most were athletic sandals and flip-flops, so not much room for spider caves anyway. Before I started looking at them, I peeked out at the lake to make sure she wasn't on her way back. She was. I could see her at the halfway point on the lake, and I figured I had at least ten minutes before she got her board out of the water and made her way up the hill.

The shoes were tiny, like the footprints from the dock. I started turning them over one by one to match the pattern from the photo on my phone. No match. Of course, a guilty person would throw the shoes away, or hide them. I walked around the cabin perimeter, peeking under the stilts that held the front side of her cabin up. There was an old rotting boat, a couple of scuppers piled together, and lots and lots of leaves. I wasn't about to go in there—spiders and snakes.

When I made it back to my spot on the lake, there was no sign of Therese, only her board sitting on the dock.

CHAPTER 21

It was past two by the time I went looking for Jack. He was taking my request for space seriously. I took the trail past Roz and Therese's cabin and was about to turn up the hill when I heard Delia shout out from her patio.

"Hey, Lee." She dropped her towel and walked toward me. "I'm still so freaked out by what happened. I mean, how can that happen here? And there's a murderer still out there. I really want to leave, but Randy won't go because of Jacob's lifeguarding job."

"Strange days indeed," I agreed. Although I wasn't as stoned as I had been on the dock an hour before, I was feeling pretty mellow and was a little bit embarrassed by my words. I was also suddenly mesmerized by how pretty Delia looked—her nervous nature distracted you from her looks, so it was only in the silence that you noticed it. Her head was covered with tiny, perfect little ringlets that kept their shape even though they were long. Most of the time she pulled them back from her flawless bronze face. She had a runner's body and was wrapped in a sports tank and shorts. I'd often seen her jogging on the camp road or down the highway.

How did she end up with Randy again?

"Do you think it happened while we were at Johnson Camp?" she asked me.

"Possibly. I didn't hear a thing that night. You?"

"I did hear someone walking around later, but I think it was Therese," she said.

"What time was that do you think?"

She thought for a moment. "What time do you think we got back? It was about ten minutes later."

"We got back at around ten."

"I'm guessing she was just headed to the bathrooms."

"How do you know it was her?" I asked.

"Well I don't really, but who else is up here?"

There wouldn't be any reason for anyone to be on that trail at night unless they were either going to or from one of the cabins or heading down to the lake from the pavilion.

"Well, I have to find my husband," I said, continuing my walk.

"See you tonight?" she asked.

"Yep. We'll be there." I walked away before she could ask me what I was bringing. People took a lot of pride in what miracles they could pull off in their tiny kitchens. We would bring a pizza from town like we always did.

Henry and Jack were in the pavilion, telling stories while they watched the lake like they were waiting for a ship to sail in. I found them by following their laughter. A small cooler of beer sat in between their chairs. I plopped down next to them, and Jack opened a beer and handed it to me without saying a word.

"I could use one of your caramels about now," Henry said.

"So could I, but I'm too lazy to go back down to camp," I replied.

Jack stood up.

"Really? You are going to get me my weed?" I asked.

"Yes, stoners, I will get you your weed. You see, I am not a stoner, so I have the energy to do it," he joked.

"Yes, drinking beer gives you so much energy." I laughed. "I may just stay as high as I can for the next week," I said to Henry.

"You should keep your wits about you just a little, Lee. After all, there is a murderer running around here." It was Detective Harris, who had to have heard everything.

Jack had already stood up to go to the cabin and threw me a look like he would be the next to commit murder. I looked over my shoulder to see the detective and tried to change the subject.

"Hey, Detective Harris! Have you met my husband, Jack, yet?"

"No. Nice to meet you." he reached out to Jack, and they both smiled as they shook hands.

"Are you any closer to finding out who did this?" Jack asked him.

"We've got some ideas," he replied. "Before you go on your bender, Lee, I was hoping to talk to you about something?" He had a grin on his face, and I couldn't help but laugh.

"Don't believe what you hear, Detective, I do my best thinking while under the influence," I replied.

He shook his head. "Would you mind stepping into my office?"

Henry and Jack were looking at me like I was about to be hauled off to jail. I didn't want anyone at camp to know I was helping him.

Harris must have sensed my discomfort. "I'm going to be talking to everyone in camp with a second round of questions. I'm hoping people remember something more now that a little time has passed. Maybe I can catch up with you next, Mr. Levine. Seems like good timing." He smiled and walked off toward the common room, and I followed, looking back at the guys with a shrug and a smile.

"Thanks for not giving me away back there," I said to him as I took a seat at his makeshift desk, which was a six-foot-long folding table in front of the big stone fireplace.

The room was meant for great camp-style celebrations. The high vaulted ceilings had logs for beams, and the enormous fireplace mantle was lined with trophies from races as far back as 1930. Some were dented. One looked as if it took too much heat and melted out of shape. They all were black with tarnish and covered with dust. Black-and-white group photos of winning teams of past paddlers hung about the walls. There was a bookshelf filled with games and puzzles with lots of loose pieces and duplicates. Two full sides of the great room had windows, and through the trees, you could see the lake below. The room smelled like burnt firewood.

"So what do we know?" he asked.

"What do you know?" I asked.

"I asked first," he said.

I smiled at him. The tiny creases around his eyes and mouth gave him away—he could only play good cop. I thought of young Officer Lars Carter. He would always play bad cop. Lars looked like a guy who would give his own mother a ticket.

"Hmm. Where to start?" I sighed. "I've discovered quite a bit of motive. The woman was making enemies all over the lake."

"Let's go down the list. Roz and Moe Martin?"

"Roz and Moe couldn't hurt a..." I stopped myself. "Oh, I did find out that Emily was a blackmailer."

"Blackmail?" He raised his brows. "Now it's getting interesting."

"She was blackmailing people in camp. One I know of for sure."

He waited for me to finish. I was having a hard time getting it past my lips.

"Bobby Richfield." Then I added quickly, "But he didn't do it."

"What did she have on him?" he asked.

"She took a video of him doing some labor intensive work around camp. He's on disability. She threatened to send the footage in to someone. Whom would you even send that to?"

"He could lose his income and possibly be prosecuted if he isn't really injured. It's fraud. That's as real a motive as any," he said.

"He is injured. The guy lives on painkillers," I said, feeling like I had to defend Bobby—then realizing that it didn't help him at all. "That's not all. I saw Bobby at Emily's cabin the morning we found her." I knew he wasn't going to like this.

"And you're telling me now because?" He wasn't a happy camper.

"Because I wanted to give him the benefit of the doubt. I wanted to talk to him about it first before I said anything," I said, waiting for Harris to yell at me.

"Ms. Harding, what makes you think he would tell you if he committed murder? People tend to keep that close to the chest." He was disturbed but restrained. I noticed he'd gone back to calling me "Ms. Harding." Not a good sign.

"I get that. I do. It's just, well, Bobby is so pathetic. I just…"

"Did you know that he was suspected of stealing camp funds for years?" he asked.

"What? Who told you that?" I didn't believe it.

"Marge Rice told me. That's the reason he was fired as camp director some years back. The Board didn't want the scandal. They were afraid they would lose their lease. So the police weren't called, but it came close," he told me.

"I told you to watch out for Marge," I said. "Why would she try to implicate Bobby when he so often works as her servant? He'll do anything for her." I stood up and paced in front of his desk. "And that doesn't make him a murderer. Look, what he told me was that he went there to look for Emily's phone, so he could delete the video from it. But when he opened the door, the place was already upside down, so he left, and that's when I saw him. He wasn't coming out of the cabin; he was just closing the door. And I can tell you that he wasn't wearing gloves or anything, so if he is lying, you should find his fingerprints all over. He's not a neat guy."

"Anyway," I said, trying to get him to move on. "She never asked Bobby for money. I think she had a cabin in mind. I think she was collecting secrets to maneuver herself into a cabin lease," I told him. "The politics involved in getting a cabin are just ridiculous. I wouldn't be surprised if we found out that's what this is all about."

"People get murdered for less," he said. "So we have at least one person being blackmailed, and we have three groups of people whose cabin leases were up." He was thinking out loud.

"Randy Foster is also in the lottery. Is someone going to try to kill him too?" I asked.

"Well, let's just hope this was about blackmail, Lee. The last thing I need is another murder."

"Freddie has no motive. He's perfectly happy in the bunkhouse," I added.

"Unless she was blackmailing him too." Harris looked up at me to see if I knew anything. He was watching my face, like the cop that he was.

"I doubt Emily could even find Freddie to blackmail him. He's like a bear. You don't see him until you cook something."

"Should I even ask if you're going to tell me anything else you learn?" he asked.

"Anything I find out that's relevant to this case, I will tell you," I promised. "By the way, those flip-flop tracks down at the dock… Therese keeps her shoes outside of the cabin. They look about the right size."

"I already have the shoes that made those marks. I've sent them to the county forensics team," he told me as he shuffled through some papers.

"Did you find them in front of her cabin?" I asked.

"Sure did. They'd been cleaned up for the most part."

"What did Therese say?"

"She said she hadn't worn them in a while. Claimed they caused blisters. She said she isn't stupid; if she'd stepped in blood, she would have cleaned them with bleach or tossed 'em," he said.

"That makes sense. I mean, who puts them right back where they were?"

"Someone wanted it to look like Therese was on the dock that night," he said. I nodded in agreement as I left the room.

A cold beer awaited me in the pavilion. Jack and Henry were talking about recovery maneuvers, and between that and the afternoon silence that blanketed the camp, I was lulled into a chair nap.

CHAPTER 22

THE SKY HAD DARKENED TO the time of day when sunbathers pack it up and the lifeguard gets a first chance to open a book. The stairs down to the dock were various heights and lengths. In some places a large rock substituted for a manmade stair. I made my way down, switching from side to side on the steeper steps. The brush on both sides of the path was dense and constantly competing with the trail. I heard a rustle in the leafy bed that startled me. It was a chipmunk and not a snake as I had feared.

"Hi, Jake," I called out as I stepped onto the decking.

"Hey," he said with a typical teenage lack of enthusiasm.

"No customers today?" I asked, walking past him and to the dock's edge.

"Not yet. I usually get some afternoon swimmers though," he said. "Emily always swam at four."

"Death is pretty strange, isn't it?" I said without looking for a response. "I mean she was here, and now she is just gone. Poof!"

"I'm pretty used to it. I lost my mom and my grandma."

I'd known Jake for the last five years, and had only known Delia as his mother. But I knew their story.

He hung out with my boys when they were here. They were summer friends. Together with Luanne's girls, the group of them would get into all kinds of trouble around camp. Good trouble, like trying to rock a loose dock until some of the kids fell off or battling each other in scupper wars. They swam and chased and talked about their young lives all day and into the night. When they would finally return to the cabin, they slept like dirt-covered rocks.

"I lost both of my parents by the time I was ten. It's still very difficult. I miss them every day," I told him. I sat down and dipped my legs into the water. It was warm, and I was tempted to jump in but didn't feel like dealing with a wet bathing suit at that time of day.

"I didn't know that," he said. And then a few moments later added, "Wow, both parents. Who took care of you?"

"My sisters. Well, my oldest sister really. She dropped out of college and came home to raise me. I was lucky to have her." We were bonded by similar experience for a moment—both of us remembering our shared pain in silence.

"What did you think of Emily?" I asked Jacob.

"She was all right, I guess…mostly nice to me. She complained a lot. Everything always hurt." He was quiet, like he remembered something, and wore a half smile. "Did you ever see her in her swim gear?"

"No, but I can imagine."

"Yeah, full goggles and snorkel, flippers, and a plastic fanny pack! That was kind of cool, really. It was waterproof, and she listened to music on this old-fashioned CD thing while she swam. I didn't even know you could do that."

"A Walkman?" I asked, laughing.

He shrugged. "I guess that's what it's called."

I wondered how I had gotten so old.

Two figures were coming down the hill. When I looked up to see who it was, Jacob turned around to take a look.

"Marge and Lester. They swim every day too," he said without enthusiasm.

"Every day at four?" I asked.

"Usually," he replied.

"So they swam with Emily. Were they friends?" I asked.

He nodded. "I don't think Marge liked her. No surprise there. But Emily and Lester got along pretty well."

They hadn't been seen outside their cabin since the morning of the murder, so I didn't want to miss this opportunity, especially since I'd heard they might be leaving later.

"Oh, I'm glad you're here, Lee," Marge said. "When are you going to join the Board?" She didn't acknowledge Jacob. She was always asking me to join the board of directors, and I was always saying no. There was no way I would step into that pile of political dung. Luanne had shared far too many stories.

"It's just not possible with all I have going on," I replied.

If she were kind, she would have been beautiful. Her creamy white skin had aged well. I'd never seen her without a hat. Her one-piece suit was modest and expensive, hanging just right on her thin frame. I imagined her to be a woman whose family once had money.

Her brother was standing next to her, trying to unfold one of the beach chairs he'd carried down. She went to help him, but he dropped it and jumped in the water, ignoring her offer.

"He's not himself," she said with condescending apology.

Lester appeared older than her, small and weak in stature. Marge treated him as if he were her child. We watched as he swam out to the dock, climbed up the ladder, and lay down on his back, as if he'd escaped her safely and could relax. I wondered what he was thinking.

"I heard you guys are leaving tonight," I said, hoping to get her talking about Emily.

"I wanted to get out of here after that terrible business with Emily, but Lester won't go. He just refuses." She rolled her eyes as if I would understand.

"Were you friendly with Emily?" I asked.

"I hardly knew the woman," she said as though disgusted at the thought of her.

I thought of what Jacob had just told me. If Marge and Emily were on the dock at the same time, there was no way in the world Emily wouldn't talk to her.

"She was pretty hard to ignore," I said. "I only met her a few times, but she left a pretty lasting impression."

"That's a nice way of putting it," she said and opened a hardcover biography of Margaret Thatcher, signaling that our conversation was over.

CHAPTER 23

IT WAS A STRANGE NIGHT for a potluck. Strings of round bulbs swung
from the logs that served as headers for the pavilion. The bulbs cast
their little shadows, making a pattern across the floor. Luanne had
lined up two long folding tables to eat family style and another two
tables for the potluck. They were covered with checkered tablecloths
decorated with jars of freshly picked Mountain Laurel and candles.

Everyone in camp showed up with foil-wrapped meals served in
chipped bowls that were no longer good enough at home. The excep-
tions were Roz's two dishes, which came in a clay pots worthy of only
the best kitchen, and Marge and Lester's box of previously opened
crackers and a bar of cheddar, for which they did not even bring a
plate or a knife. Luanne ended up slicing and plating the cheese, and
her annoyance did not go unnoticed.

The forensics team had wrapped up their work in Emily's cabin
and car and had left together just a few minutes earlier. There was
no police presence in the pavilion that night, and for a while we all
pretended like death had never come to camp.

I'd sent Jack down to the Road House to pick up a pasta dish and
then threw it in a bowl from the cabin. No one was fooled, but they
ate it gladly. Luanne brought her famous lentils, and Roz had made

two separate stews, one vegetable with rice for me, and the other with meat. There were salads and bread and lots of bottles of wine.

"Where is that detective tonight?" Randy asked.

"Lars Carter's been assigned to stay in camp until this mess is settled," Luanne told us. She returned to cutting her food as we all tried not to look at each other. Her statement was a reminder that all of us were considered suspects in Emily's murder. When the chatter picked up again, wine glasses seemed to empty at a faster rate than usual.

After dinner, Maddy plugged in a portable speaker and played Lou Rawls's, "You'll Never Find." Henry stood up and reached his hand out to her, and the two danced together as if they were alone. Roz and Moe ended up joining them in the empty space in front of the fireplace, which then served as a dance floor. Jack looked at me, and I quickly turned away as if I hadn't noticed. Lester sat to my right and seemed to be moping over his plate. It was hard to tell since he rarely ever spoke to me.

"What's going on, Lester? Are you okay?" I asked him.

"A woman died. People are acting like she didn't matter," he said quietly as if he would be in trouble if he were heard. He looked over at his sister, who was chatting away with Delia, and then back down at his plate as if afraid.

"Maybe they just need a few moments to forget," I suggested.

My glass was empty, and the bottle in front of me was too. I rose to get another off the banquet table. As I stood opening it, Jacob Foster came to my side.

"She lied to you today," he said.

"Who lied to me?" I asked.

"Marge. She knew Emily. Emily and Lester had swum together every day for weeks. They really liked each other. It was like watching two little kids. Marge tried to change the time they went to the swim docks, but Lester wouldn't have it."

"Why wouldn't Marge want Lester to have a friend? It seems like it would be a relief for her to not have to care for him all of the time."

When I looked over at Marge, she was watching us. She was wearing an apple-green sweater with a pink shift beneath it. The sweater hung around her shoulders and was held together with a pearl button. A pair of glasses dangled from the long gold chain around her neck. She diverted her eyes quickly when she saw me glance back at her.

The music picked up, and several of us were dancing when Detective Harris and Carter came back to camp. Harris was looking our way, and for a moment, his eyes met mine. I didn't care. I danced with my girlfriends, freely and with joy.

I'd worn my favorite white summer dress with its long flowing skirt and chain of daisies around the neckline. Jack's hungry eyes were on me, but I ignored them. I danced for me — dancing away the despair of the past few days. Maddy grabbed my arm and spun me around so quickly that I had a hard time holding my head up. As the world whirled by, I danced to forget.

Campers wandered out, some saying goodnight, some slipping quietly into the darkness. Soon it was just me, alone with the music, the lights, and the darkness beyond the pavilion. And Jack (who had assured Lu that he would shut everything down) sitting with his beer in hand, watching me dance with my eyes closed.

I resented him for being here. He hadn't been invited. I'd come alone, and I wanted to dance alone. His presence also reminded me that Carter was trying to sleep in the great room across from us, and even though the music was low, it was time to leave. Jack always did the right thing. It was easy for him.

We walked back to the cabin single file in the dark, every bump and curve familiar to us. The only light in camp came from Roz and

Moe's cabin. I smiled at the thought of my nocturnal forest friends. They really were like little woodland creatures.

As soon as the screen door closed behind us, Jack took me by the wrist and spun me toward him.

"Why don't you tell me just what exactly I have done to make you dislike me so deeply?" He was calm, but I could sense in his voice hurt and anger, which are often the same. The realization that I could wound him caused me great pain, and I began to cry. It was easier for me to stay angry. But I couldn't be mad at him anymore because he was kind and he loved me, and I loved him too, through the resentment and unhappy moments. I started to sob, trying to be quiet because every clanging dish could be heard in the darkness of the camp. I couldn't talk, and he pulled me close to comfort me even thought I was the one causing him pain. When the tears subsided, I fell asleep with his arms wrapped around me in our tiny bedroom with its tiny bed.

When I woke up several hours later, it was the first moments of dawn, that brief time when all things natural sleep together. I removed Jack's arm from around my waist and climbed from the bed quietly. Grabbing a blanket that had fallen to the floor, I slipped into my flip-flops and out the door and took the path down to the dock. In the short time since I had opened my eyes, the birds had awakened and the forest was beginning to echo with their airborne chatter. The splash of the loose ramp startled me as I stepped on, but I kept my balance. The spot where Emily had died seemed to glow with death.

A dense fog sat on the lake, steam-like and mystical. The water had a light yellow dusting of pollen on its surface. An occasional fish jumped, disturbing the coating and revealing the glasslike water beneath it. In the dawn, the lake was a bayou in mourning, humid and silent.

I sat in one of the two chairs I'd left there and took a deep breath, exhaling slowly. My head hurt from my sins of the night before. My body was calling for coffee. Before long the lake would rise and sink the pollen with awakening wind. Soon the tree-topped mountains of the great Hudson Valley were black silhouettes against the deep orange announcement of the coming sun.

As the light of the day conquered the mist, I rose to do some stretching, but my head screamed, *No.* Instead I played my favorite Decembrists song, "Rise to Me," and closed my eyes to listen. Jack stepped onto the dock with two mugs in his hand.

"Oh my God, you read my mind!" I moaned, sitting up to grab the hot cup of heaven. He didn't say a word as he handed it to me, and I remembered the evening before with some shame.

"Sometimes I think you are going to make me pay for the rest of my life," he said, looking out at the lake like he was speaking to it. His free hand was in his pocket, and he stood straight, as he always did, as he was told to from the time he took his first step. There was sadness in his voice. And regret. While I stared at his square jaw, I thought about my little Max and how much he looked like his father. Only now, instead of the confident man I'd married, it was the father that resembled his young son's vulnerability. It hurt my heart.

"This isn't about that," I said, trying to be gentle, as if I were talking to my child. "That" was always his early indiscretion in our marriage. "I just don't know if we share the same dreams anymore, Jack. I want so much more than a big house and a sports car. I want to make a difference here on this planet. I want my kids to value what they do for others over what they get for themselves. I don't think that's what is going to make you happy."

"I know what is not going to make me happy. I know that life without you will bring me a lifetime of sadness. I know that tearing my kids' family life apart will make me unhappy. Is this what you want? All because I don't want to live in Africa?" he asked incredulously.

"It's not about Africa, Jack. It's about values. You're driving the boys to be like you…and your father. I don't want that life for them." My voice was getting too high with anger and lies because in some ways it *was* about Africa, or anywhere else I wanted to run away to. There could never be spontaneous adventure with this man. It just wasn't in his DNA.

"Oh, you've never screwed up? You're a perfect parent, right? How long before our kids know that you are regularly buzzed to get through life? Do I hold that against you?" He waited for my response. I gave him my evil eye, squinty and dagger-like. "Oh, and then there's your little detective boyfriend in San Francisco. I put up with a lot, Lee."

"I don't get high in front of my kids. That's my time!" I stood up, angry and pacing. "My time! And how is that different from you coming home after not seeing them at all and drinking half a bottle of wine?" I was trying to keep my voice down, but I was blindly angry. "I know I'm not a perfect parent," I whispered. "But it's the values, Jack. You love money! Your parents love money! I want my kids to love something else."

"I love providing my family with security and the things they enjoy, yes. I love that my wife can take off to just about anywhere in the world she wants when she needs to. I love that my kids can go to the best summer camps. And why don't you cut the shit? So do you." He stood up and faced me. There we were, in one of my favorite places in the world, now stained with blood and tears and anger.

"Can we not do this here? This is not the place to do this." I looked around to see if anyone had heard us.

"I'll wait for you to get through this, Lee, but not forever," he said and left me alone, with a cup of cold coffee and head full of confusion and sorrow.

CHAPTER 24

Roz returned from her morning paddle as I sat stunned on the dock. I had wiped my tears when I saw her coming and was pretending to be fine by the time she pulled her boat up. She was outfitted in a khaki fishing vest—its pockets bulging with supplies for her daily adventures—and a floppy rayon sun hat. I offered to help her out, but she refused.

"I've been doing this for a long time. It's good for me to keep at it," she said. "What are you doing up so early?"

"I wanted some solitude."

She fiddled with some rigging and pulled her boat onto the dock, rinsing the pollen off of the bottom of her boat while I sat watching. "You okay?"

"I'm fine," I lied, wiping the tears that her question triggered. "Jack and I are having a tough time. I came up here to have some thinking time, but he insisted on coming after what happened with Emily."

"Well, you've come this far. I'm sure you'll be fine," she said casually. "I spent a summer alone up here once. Right after my youngest moved out. I wasn't sure I wanted to be married anymore. I had never even lived on my own before—got married when I was eighteen.

Went from my father tellin' me what to do to my husband tellin' me." She laughed.

"So what changed your mind?" I asked.

"It hurt too much to live without him."

I understood that. Jack's pain was hurting me more than my own. I knew it was time to end this charade. I couldn't leave him if I tried. Not because of the kids, but because our love went deeper than romance or location or anything else. We were a part of each other.

"Have a good day, Roz," I said, heading up to my cabin. I walked back, thinking of the words I would say to Jack, but he wasn't there. I searched the pavilion. It was still early, and camp was silent. I went down to the swim docks. The steam from the lake was rising with the morning.

Stan the turtle was on the shoreline by the ramp, where I had never seen him before. I'd heard he sunned on the dock but had never been lucky enough to spot him there. I stayed on the ramp, a little afraid of him. He was so large, the size of a kitchen sink. His beak was open, as if he was talking, and I thought he might be trying to scare me off. I stayed where I was, but he still didn't move. I walked a little closer and saw that there was something hanging from his neck. Worried that he was stuck on something, I looked around for a stick and walked closer.

There was no hissing or backing away. Stan was dead. Someone had wrapped a yellow plastic rope around his neck and tied it tightly into a knot. I tried to get it off, but it was too late. He was suspended in his last gasping breath.

I ran back to camp to get help, throwing the door to the great room open.

"I think you'd better come with me," I said to Lars Carter, who was dressed in a T-shirt and sweat pants. "Someone's killed Stan!" I cried. I explained between sobs what I had found as he followed me down to the swim area.

"Who would do this?" Carter asked like a sad child.

I remembered that he grew up here and Stan was a part of his world too. I could only shake my head as tears filled both of our eyes.

CHAPTER 25

JACK WAS NOWHERE TO BE found that day.

Apparently, he'd run into Henry, and the two of them had taken off hiking. I felt like I deserved to be left behind, and I paced all day waiting for him to get back, desperately wanting to tell him about Stan.

I sat down on the swim dock with my feet hanging into the water, feeling like Atlas with the world on my shoulders. My concerns that Stan would think my toes were fish and bite them were no more. I was angry and sad, but mostly angry. I'd found a branch of mountain laurel and was pushing it back and forth in mourning, announcing Stan's parting to the underwater world. I spent the day occupying my-self with the death, asking myself who would do such a thing. Was it related to Emily's death? According to Harris, Emily had been pushed into the boat rack with quite a bit of force. If that was a crime of pas-sion or an accident, though, why kill the turtle? Stan's death had been clearly deliberate and malicious. I couldn't get his anguished look out of my mind—his open beak frozen in a final gasp for air. Anger was quickly becoming stronger than sadness again.

I'd stashed a joint in my bra earlier and pulled it out and lit it. I took a deep hit, exhaling as I heard the footsteps coming down the hill. I smashed it on the surface of the dock to put it out and tucked it neatly back where it had come from. Soon Detective Jed Harris's boots were standing next to me.

"You okay?"

I looked up at him, hand over my face as the afternoon sun began its ascent over his head. I was aware that the air around me was thick and sweet, and I knew that he knew what I had been up to. Thank goodness he was here for a murder.

"I'm okay. I'm super fucking pissed, but I'm okay."

"It's a terrible thing," he agreed more politely.

"It's worse than killing Emily, that's for sure. It's a bigger loss to the world." I felt bad immediately after I spoke.

Harris laughed a little uncomfortably. "From what I've learned about the woman, you're probably right."

"Poor Emily. I shouldn't take Stan's death out on her. But he was an innocent," I said. We were quiet for a moment, both of us staring across the lake at nothing in particular. "Why have you shared so much about the case with me?" I finally asked him.

He thought a few seconds and said, "Because I trust you."

"Why?" I asked him.

"Because you don't rip me off with lies."

I liked Harris a lot. He was good all the way through, like children and dogs. I had hardly ever met people that good.

"So let me ask you something. It's kind of personal and off the record," he said.

"All right. Ask away."

"I know a few people who smoke pot, and they all hide if from me, probably because I'm in law enforcement. One of my sons smokes— he thinks I don't know. What's so great about pot?"

"You've never tried it?" I asked.

He shook his head.

"I can help with that," I joked. Thinking of the joint in my cleavage made me giggle. He looked scared for a moment, and I took pity on him. "I started using pot after I developed an allergy to Advil. The doctor told me it was steroids or nothing in the anti-inflammatory world. So when a friend told me that weed worked well for inflammation, I gave it a shot. That's when I figured out that it could also take the edge off of life for me. Kind of like Xanax, only nature gave it to us instead of a lab. So your wife didn't use it when she was sick?" I asked. "It's really great for nausea."

"Danny, our youngest, brought a little bag over when she was sick, but she was afraid of getting high," he explained.

I thought about the morphine and anti-anxiety medications people are given during hospice. They get you incredibly high, but people still feared weed. I knew it was useless to bring it up.

"Well, maybe I'll try it when it's legal. I'll be a retired pothead," he chuckled.

"Really? I'd like to see that," I laughed. "Okay, my turn to ask you a question."

"Ask away."

"Think you'll ever remarry?"

"No," he answered decisively.

"You must have loved her very much." I was picking the leaves off of the branch and throwing them into the lake one by one.

"We had twenty-eight wonderful years together—some hard times, some real hard times—but we always loved and cared for each other. I can't imagine going through all that getting to know each other again. I dated here and there, and I have a friend I hang out with some times. That's good enough." He paused. "That's a nice husband you have there. I can see that he cares deeply for you."

"Yeah, well, it's been one of those hard times," I said, eyes welling.

"This too shall pass." He stood there for what seemed like a while longer. Then he helped me onto my feet, and we walked back up to the camp in silence.

I took a nap and woke in a still-empty cabin. I decided to walk out to the highway to see if Jack was on his way back. It was getting dark, and I figured they would have to return soon. I chose the path we'd used when he'd come into camp, thinking it would be his preferred trail. As I approached Bobby's cabin, I heard voices and slowed down to listen. I turned the corner and saw Luanne at Bobby's door, pointing and yelling, and he was backing away like she was about to hit him.

"Whoa. Luanne. You okay?" I said as I came closer.

"Ask this muthuh fuckuh," she said and stormed past me.

Bobby shut the door before I had a chance to speak.

There was no sign of Jack on the trail. I was starting to think he'd given up on me and gone home. My heart was heavy as I tried to figure out what to do next. I shot up the hill on a narrow trail that led to the tent platforms and campsites that were now vacant. The more I thought of Stan and Jack and Emily, the faster I walked, until soon I was running up the hill, sweating and gasping, but I couldn't stop myself. All of the anger I'd felt that day started to fall down the trail behind me as I worked harder and harder to reach the top.

I was panting heavily when I reached the crest and stood there holding my sides while I caught my breath.

A voice came from within the woods, gentle and familiar. "Hello, Lee."

I smiled and wiped my damp brow as I walked over to a tent platform where Freddie sat like Gandhi, his legs tied up in a pretzel.

"Hey, Freddie. Sorry to disturb your quiet."

"I'm never unhappy to see you. Would you like to practice some meditation?"

"I'm no good at it," I said, shaking my head.

He laughed.

"I'm serious. Why do you think I smoke so much weed? I can't stay still, never could. And making my mind shut up is nearly impossible…unless I medicate."

"Buddha said that there are only two mistakes one can make along the road to truth: not going all the way, and not starting." He smiled. "It's just a state of reflection."

"I like to move while I reflect," I told him.

He patted the platform next to him, motioning me to sit. "It will only take sixty seconds, and it won't hurt, I promise."

I sat down and tried to fold my legs like his, but I was stiff and had to force them.

"Don't worry. Be comfortable." He waited for me to wiggle and adjust.

"The problem is I can't think of nothing. It makes me giggle for some reason," I explained.

"Because you are afraid to fail. There is no wrong here, Lee. Don't attempt to not have thoughts. Instead, let them come. Observe them like an outsider. Better yet, pretend they are falling leaves, and watch them slip away." He sat straight, and I mimicked him, closing my eyes and pretending that each of my burdens; the pain of missing my kids, the fear of losing my family, the anger from Stan's death, the concern about Luanne were leaves drifting down around me.

Freddie reminded me to breathe from my stomach and then added, "Now say thank you. Be filled with gratitude."

"Thank you," I said out loud.

"Say thank you for what you have. Again and again. In your heart, Lee."

And so I let my heart be filled with gratitude for the beautiful children I had and the not-so-well-behaved dogs, for the husband who would walk through fire for me and the food that I never had to worry about getting, for warm fires and Freddie, who sat next to me so quietly, trying to help my busy mind.

CHAPTER 26

I WAS FLUSH WITH CALM. The dock was my island, the black night my camouflage. Cicadas acted as stereo and the lights on Johnson Camp were my meditative focal point. I was waiting for Tom Johnson to cross the lake. Maybe if I surprised him, he would be more willing to talk about what he knew.

I heard the sounds of footsteps coming down the path—crunching leaves and moving gravel—and assumed it was Jack. I still hadn't seen him all day and had no idea where he was. When the feet hit the ramp with a splash and the dock moved, I turned to see Lester standing there instead. He walked to the exact spot where Emily's body had been found and lowered his head as if looking for something.

"You okay, Lester?"

"It's like nobody cares she's dead," he spoke softly and in sorrow.

"You guys were friends weren't you? Swam together each day?"

"We were more than friends. We cared for each other."

"Lester, I am so sorry."

The thought of the two of them made perfect sense. Lester was rigid in his thinking. I remembered him yelling at me during the square dance one year because I do-sied when I should have doed. He was different than Emily, more absolute than demanding. Lester was different. For this I had dismissed him as weird, but I could see now, in my state of overwhelming calm, that he mattered. He was suffering from humanity like the rest of us; he just did it in a different way.

"I saw her here that night. I got scared and ran away. Maybe if I had called someone, they would have saved her. My sister said, 'No! They will think you did it.' I wouldn't hurt Emily. She was my friend."

Lester saw Emily dead on the dock that night? "Did you meet her here often?" I asked gently, like I was speaking to an upset child.

"Yes, every night, after Marge went to sleep. Every night at ten o'clock. We sat and talked and held hands. We whispered. This was our place."

This was MY place! I wanted to say, then realized that the dock was just like the cabins. They belonged to everyone. I was actually in his and Emily's special place. *I was the intruder.* I pictured the two of them meeting here, innocently—friends, sneaking away. Emily must have loved the adventure of it. In a way, she'd been as childish and clueless as Lester was. And her rigid nature was perfect for him. They could hold hands through life and follow all the rules and there would be order.

"Lester, did Marge see Emily's body that night too?" I asked.

Lester didn't reply. He turned away from me and walked back to his cabin.

Moments later, my husband plopped down into the chair beside me.

"I thought a bear had eaten you," I said flatly.

"Henry and I went to Earl's for dinner and some beers. Henry drove. Don't worry."

I could tell he'd had a few. I got out of my chair and went over to him. He put his hands in my hair, and I felt the comfort of familiarity and safety with his touch.

"Do you remember when you were pregnant with Jack and we went out to breakfast with the Philipses and their daughter was ducking under the table? How appalled I was? And I told you that no child of ours would ever be allowed to do that? And then they both did. Remember?" he laughed.

"And we got into an argument because I thought you were going to be this Nazi parent, and I questioned whether we should even be having children together." I laughed. "Yes. I remember."

"And you turned out to be the hard ass, and I'm the softie," he reminded me. "How about we let this argument about what we are going to do in the future happen when it happens?"

I curled into him, and we sat there for a few minutes. It felt so good to be in his arms. Outside of them there was death and war and violence and uncertainty, but nothing could get past him to me. I knew I could exist without him, but I also knew that I didn't want to.

He took my face in his hands and kissed me hard. He pushed out of the chair, and we tumbled onto the dock, and thus began the most passionate sex we'd ever had. The kind of lovemaking that only the familiar could have. It was intense and honest and the most adventurous thing we'd done together in years. The beavers and the turtles and the fish and the birds knew that we were animals too.

Afterwards, as we lay on our backs looking up at the stars, we held hands in silence.

"I love you," I whispered, tears flowing out both of my eyes down to my temples.

He took my hand a little tighter and said, "I'd follow you to Timbuktu."

I was grateful Tom Johnson did not appear that evening.

"Let's swim. Right here off of the dock," I said to Jack.

He was reluctant, but I knew he would because he never said no to me after sex. Never.

We lowered our naked bodies into the lake slowly, and the water enveloped us in its cool grasp. It was a clear night, not too warm, so it was a shock to my system when I got in, and I had to take several deep breaths to tell my body that it was okay.

I floated on my back, staring into the black sky as billions of tiny stars reminded me that I was nothing, not even a speck in the universe, smaller than a grain of sand.

"Emily had a Walkman. She rigged a waterproof system for it with a plastic bag and packing tape," I whispered to Jack, who had begun to swim away.

This time it didn't bother me to be left behind with my own thoughts. I could hear a banjo, and the words of my favorite Guster song filled my head.

Looks like these afternoons of reverie are through
What's left for me to say, what's left for me to do?
Float along and feel the water on back
Try not to sink down to the bottom

The banjo continued to strum as my body floated to the gently rhythm of the lake. The magnificence of the sky beamed a joy that was unimaginable just a few hours ago. I was naked before the universe. My hair was fanned out around me like silken feathers; only my chin and nose touched the summer air. The dark water reflected the starlight on its surface, and I imaged myself out there in the universe, floating naked and truthful and empty of heartache.

Hollow my head, it echoes like a wooden drum
Peel back my skin and make my ribs a xylophone
Feel the water rise and fall between my bones
And then just sink down to the bottom

I realized that I didn't need Jack to feel the same and do the same things I did. We were sharing the magnificence of the night intimately, and yet uniquely. He allowed me to be me, and it was time to give him the same courtesy.

CHAPTER 27

STAN WAS SWIMMING IN THE muddy shallows where the mossy hill dropped off like a tiny cliff and the water was clear and the bottom held perfectly shaped leaves and debris from the overhanging trees. He found a slope and crawled out of the water toward me. There was a moment of fear, but I was so happy to see him that I could only rejoice, saying, "Stan! You're alive! They didn't kill you." His crawl was slow but strong, and when he got to my feet he opened his mouth to hiss but instead released a long moan, like a foghorn. I awoke in fear and realized the air horn for the regatta was blowing.

"Shit!" Jack said, jumping out of bed and throwing on his swimsuit and flip-flops. "I told Henry I would work safety for the regatta." He leaned over and kissed me softly on the cheek.

Every year in July, the many camps of Harriman State Park descended on Lake Montego for a youth regatta. Girls clad in team T-shirts and braids raced boys with braces and acne across a marked distance on the lake. Camp counselors and volunteers sat under canopies and recorded wins, cheering on their teams as if it were the Olympics. It was tradition, and Harriman was thick with it.

"I have three huge mosquito bites on my ass thanks to you," I mumbled.

He patted them quickly and rushed out, the screen door slamming behind him. I hadn't even told him about Stan yet. He didn't know that the park supervisor had come and taken him away. A fresh new morning wave of anger washed over me. I was going to find out who killed Stan, and then I was going to punch them in the face.

I made coffee and took it with me to the pavilion to watch the races. The parking lot would normally be cluttered with cars full of paddlers gearing up for the regatta. Montego always had a strong group of competitors, kids and adults alike. Teams from all over the park descended on the shores for this race. Normally, a group from our camp would paddle over to the beach together, showing our strength in numbers and reminding the others that it was our home turf. The only person in the lot this morning was Detective Harris.

"Just the person I was looking for." He smiled.

"This is just sad," I said. "This is usually an exciting day in camp." I held my hands out to the deserted parking lot. "Not that I don't like the quiet, but…"

Camp was silent.

"Well, with everyone gone, we can talk openly. Do you have some time?"

"Nothing but." I smiled and followed him to the great room.

Officer Carter was waiting for us when we got there. His cot, tucked and without a wrinkle, was made up as neatly as if his drill sergeant were coming. We said our good mornings and got to business. I told Harris about my conversation with Lester last night.

"So let me get this straight, you were sitting in the dark on the exact spot that Emily was killed, waiting for a suspect to show up? Are you out of your mind?" It was the first time I'd seen Harris angry. He was not scary.

"He never showed," I said, shrugging. I hadn't mentioned that I'd had to get seriously high to find the courage to go there. "Maybe

Marge somehow did it. I mean, let's say she figured out that Emily and Lester were meeting up. Maybe she went down to the dock to tell Emily to lay off, and when she refused, Marge pushed her?"

"Let's go chat with the Rices," Harris said.

"So you want to go to the regatta?" I said. "That's where they are. Marge always works as a scorekeeper. Lester loves the races. He paces the beach in the direction the boats are rowing and shouts at them the whole time." A smile came over me as I thought of Lester. Why had I never see it before? "My guess is that Lester has Asperger's," I said. "I feel terrible that I never considered it before, probably because of his age. I only think of kids as having it. People always write him off as weird. He's actually very sweet. It makes me sad that someone took his chance for love away. I hope it wasn't that nasty sister of his."

I could hear the whistles blowing from across the lake and wanted to watch the regatta. "Do you need me? I want to go watch from the pavilion." I pointed toward the door.

"Nah, go ahead. Thanks for the heads up."

"Can I go with you when you talk to the Rices?"

Carter was shaking his head, about to say no, when Harris answered, "I don't see why not."

I left before he could change his mind. When I got to the pavilion, I saw Moe hanging out in one of the Adirondack chairs facing the lake. Over the low bark-covered railing of the pavilion there was a clearing in the trees, perfect for watching the races. The water was littered with kayaks, one of which would be Jack, ready to rescue racers when they tipped in their heavy canoes. The grassy treeless shoreline was cluttered with pop-up canopies and people.

Moe had a plate of sliced and diced fruit, a muffin, and a thermos, which I hoped was coffee. I thanked Roz in my head.

"Hey, Moe! No Regatta for you today?"

"No, not this year. My bursitis is killing me. Roz is over there keeping score though. Want some fruit? Coffee?"

I thanked him and took him up on the offer, refilling my mug and settling in next to him. I wanted to tell him that I had just the thing for his bursitis, but people of his generation had been convinced by years of propaganda. Even Sanjay Gupta couldn't change their minds about the medicinal benefits of cannabis.

"Why aren't you over there?" he asked.

"My heart isn't in it without the boys. I'm missing them like crazy. They only let us talk to them once a week. It's killing me." I ached just thinking about them.

"I know the feeling," he said.

"Poor Moe. Well, you have us."

"Maybe not for long," he answered. "Our lease is up. If we don't win the lottery, we're hanging it up."

"What? No way. This place would never be the same without you two," I said. But I knew I was patronizing him. Roz and Moe couldn't do a rental cabin. It would be too much work to haul everything back and forth; that was a task for young people. The older couple would come less and less, until one summer they wouldn't show up at all. He looked sad, and I patted his shoulder. "You'll get your cabin. No one will let that happen to you," I said, wanting to believe in my own words.

"Well, our chances went up with Emily's death," he added.

He was right, but I couldn't believe he'd said it out loud. Moe and Roz had stayed behind the evening of Emily's death. Officially, they were on Harris's suspect list. They had both motive and opportunity. I hated that murder intruded on my feelings about my lake friends. When you only see people for a few weeks out of the year, you idealize them.

"Moe, do you know why anyone would kill Stan?"

He looked at me like he wanted to speak up but didn't answer.

"Do you know something?" I asked, looking him in the eye.

He sat quietly for a moment, then said, "I don't know anything."

"Moe, if you know something, you should tell me." I stood up and tried not to let my temper explode on the kind man.

"I don't know anything, honey. I'm sorry." He looked away when he spoke.

I sat down again but was too frustrated with him to stay and left without saying goodbye.

Red was waiting for me by the dock, and I took her out. I paddled hard and fast, thinking about why anyone would do something so cruel to such a beautiful creature. Moe knew something. I was sure of it. I stayed away from the Regatta, heading toward Johnson Beach and the cove that lay beyond it.

The church ladies had taken over the beach again. I paddled close and yelled to them. "Why don't you pick up your shit so it doesn't float into the lake, ladies?"

"What?" I could hear them gasp.

"Pick up your shit! Your garbage! Your evil plastic waste!" I yelled louder this time. I was a crazy lady. That's what I had become. Maybe it was Emily—somehow her spirit had left the dock and inhabited me last night during my and Jack's sacred act. I laughed and paddled on until the anger fell away leaving a trail of evaporating bitterness.

CHAPTER 28

IT COULD HAVE BEEN FREDDIE who said, "I never found a companion that was so companionable as solitude," but it wasn't; it was Thoreau. I found it funny that Freddie paddled to the dock just as I opened my book. It was always an honor when he came to visit, as he preferred his own company to the rest of us. I understood this, and I think that was why we were friends.

"What are you reading there?" he asked.

"Walden. It seemed appropriate," I answered, holding up the book.

He was wearing a black insulated spring suit that made him look even thinner than usual. His short dreadlocks sprouted in many directions, and I thought that, if he were a cartoon, he would be a mop.

"Yes, good book. 'We can never have enough of nature.'"

It wasn't necessary to converse with Freddie. He had mastered the art of peace. Someday I would learn to embrace peace without weed, but that day was not the one. He used his paddle to station himself in front of my dock.

"Were you out on the water the night of Emily's death, Freddie?" I finally asked.

"Yes. It was a very hot night. I spied the beavers on the west side of the lake. They had two babies, did you know?"

"I did not know," I replied and made a mental note to check them out. "Did you see anyone on the dock?"

He smiled.

"Would you tell me if you had?"

"Everything will work out as it's meant to. We don't always have to chase the answers," he said.

"I'm not really sure what that means, Freddie."

"Try to be still, Lee," he said as he paddled off.

The words of Thoreau lulled me into a slumber until the heat of the midday sun shone on my face long enough to wake me. I gathered my things and started up the trail to the cabin, awaiting Jack's return like an eager young lover. I'd had flashes of our evening all day and found myself longing for my own husband, which I found to be kind of funny. When he finally returned, I hugged him tightly. He stroked my hair and held me in his arms. It felt like home.

"I heard about Stan," he said.

"I'm going to beat the crap out of the person responsible," I said. "That poor beautiful beast. All of these years of being cautious of humans, and then someone did that to him. It must have felt like a long-planned trap."

"Do they have any idea of who would do it?" he asked.

"No, but Moe knows something. He wouldn't tell me, but he knows. I'm going to find out."

"Oh boy," he said, knowing me well enough to know I would do as I promised.

"Is Luanne in camp?" I asked.

"Yes, we all paddled back together," he said.

On the walk to her cabin, I thought of her fight with Bobby. I was hoping she would tell me what had happened. She was inside when I knocked on the door. It took her a while to get there, and when she did, she held the door open just a pinch to show me she wasn't inviting me in. I'd been in Luanne's cabin many times before. It was too small for everything she had to keep in it. It contained enough beds to hold her large family, plus supplies for camp parties and her office. It was tight in there, to say the least, but this had never kept her from inviting me in.

"You okay?" I asked. She had dark circles under her eyes. "You look like you could use some sleep."

"I'm not feelin' all that good. Can I catch up with you later?"

"Of course. You know where to find me."

I walked up to the pavilion and entered Harris and Carter's headquarters. Harris was sitting by the fireplace in an old rocking chair.

"What are you doing?" I asked him.

"I'm thinking," he said.

"Oh. Want me to leave?"

"No no. I'm glad you're here. Take a seat," he offered.

"I can't sit. I've been sitting all day. I've had so many weird experiences in the last twenty-four hours." I was pacing the floor in front of his makeshift desk.

"Moe knows who killed Stan. I'll bet others do too," I said. "I think maybe Freddie knows. He gave me some weird shit about sitting still. I don't know what the fu—" I stopped myself "—what the heck he's talking about. Have you talked to him? And what about Moe and Roz? Have you talked to them? Roz goes out paddling most evenings. Are you ready to talk to the Rices? They're probably back from the regatta now." More thoughts poured out of my mouth as I paced back and forth. "I saw Luanne and Bobby fighting last night. Luanne won't talk to me today. It's like she is avoiding me or something," I said, finally slowing down. "Where's your sidekick?"

"He's taking a swim. We still haven't found Emily's phone. I have a feeling it would be a useful thing to have. Any idea where it might be?" Harris asked.

"Not a clue," I said. "Can I have a look at her cabin? Are you finished in there? Maybe another pair of eyes…"

He nodded and tossed me the key. I headed down the road to take a look, detouring to my cabin, where Jack was sprawled out asleep. I quietly grabbed a little pouch of weed and brought it with me.

I entered Emily's cabin and locked the door behind me. First I opened all of the windows, as someone had shut them. Then I lit up the unfinished joint from yesterday and inhaled deeply. As soon the calm washed over me, I went to work, starting in the kitchen and going through every shelf, removing stacks of mismatched plates and glasses, even looking inside coffee cups that said things like, "World's Best Dad." I put everything away so that it was neater than when I got there. Normally, I would be rushing the process, but the weed had helped me slow down. I was enjoying the clean up immensely since chaos makes me crazy.

The living room was the worst of it. I found some reusable bags and a large duffle. After searching through each of the bag's zipped pockets, I filled them with the personal items that were thrown everywhere. Most of her clothes were worn and smelled like mothballs. An entire bag was filled with bug repellant and bite treatments, sunblock and swim gear. Oddly enough, there were no prescription drugs. I would have thought that with all of her ailments she would have been on ten different medications. There was a Walkman in a clear plastic case. Inside, an *Abba's Greatest Hits* CD peered back at me.

I tossed countless pairs of rolled-up tube socks into another bag, thinking of how Emily had used them to protect herself from ticks while the rest of us marched around in flip-flops, exposed to any blood suckers we happened to run into. I hesitated when it came to her more intimate items. A collection of large nude-colored panties went into the bag. They looked too big for her spindly frame and screamed, "Stay away!" Her bras, pointy breasted with thick beige cross-your-heart straps, were so old that Lauren Bacall could have worn the same brand.

What had happened to the poor woman that had made her give up on all of the softness and flexibility in life and had turned her into a worshiper of the rigid? I picked up two handfuls of clothing from a pile on the floor and placed them on top of her underwear to protect her privacy. A worn navy T-shirt fell to the side, and when I picked it up, I saw that it had peeling letters that spelled "DON'T."

There were stacks and stacks of reading materials. I shook each hiking magazine and romance novel to make sure nothing was hidden in the pages. Then I packed them neatly into a bag.

A clear plastic cosmetics pouch held Avon lipstick samples. The bag was so old it had yellowed, and where it had cracked, a new piece of clear packing tape held it together. It occurred to me that I hadn't seen any tape in the room, which reminded me that something wasn't right. Where had I seen packing tape recently?

I flew out the door and jogged over to the building that housed the restrooms. Inside the little cabinet that held surplus toiletries and cleaning supplies was the tape dispenser, exactly where I'd seen it last. I was on my hands and knees, checking under the sinks, when the main door opened.

"Lose something?" Therese asked. The tone in her voice held far more accusation than her question should merit.

"Yeah," I said. "But it's not here." I stood up, washed my hands in the sink, and dried them on the skirt of my sundress.

"Thanks a lot by the way. Because of you, the police went to Johnson and questioned Tom. He wouldn't hurt Emily. He doesn't have a mean bone in his body." I felt like a child was yelling at me. I was at least a head taller than Therese. Her little bronze face was the angriest I'd ever seen on her.

"I'm sorry, Therese, but isn't it important that the police have all the facts? I mean, maybe he saw something that night that's important to finding Emily's killer. Maybe you did too…"

"Emily was standing on the docks as Tom left camp that night. He had no reason to kill her. She'd known about us for over a year."

So it was true. Part of me wanted to say, "Way to go girl!" Tom was at least ten years younger than her, and he was pretty hot. But the thought of his wife and family made me sad. I tried to push the judgment aside. One never knows what really goes on in a marriage.

"But she was blackmailing you, wasn't she?"

"No! It was what we feared, so we came up with a plan. I told her about Camp Montego and then brought her over for a tour. She loved it here, of course. It's a much nicer camp. Once she'd booked her cabin for this summer, she left us alone."

"So you were the one who introduced her to camp? Smart," I said. But I knew she was lying. Emily had wanted a cabin, and she'd known about Therese and Tom's affair. There was no way she hadn't been blackmailing them too. I started to walk out the door but took one last look behind the cabinet I'd found the tape in, and bonanza! There it was—Emily's cell phone. I grabbed it, tape and all, and headed up to Harris before Therese could ask me any questions.

CHAPTER 29

THE PHONE WAS A SURPRISINGLY modern piece of hardware for a woman like Emily. It was smooth and white and obviously expensive. It had a great camera and video capabilities. I knew because I had the exact same one. I finished cleaning up her cabin while it sat charging in an outlet by the sink. Harris sat next to me as I folded Emily's bedding into neat stacks. Then I rechecked her mattress and felt her pillow for hidden objects.

"You're right. There's nothing here," I said, resigned.

"You found her phone. The search was successful," he reminded me.

"Is it charged yet?"

"No more than it was when you asked thirty seconds ago," he chuckled.

"Need a book?" I joked. "She certainly loved her romance novels." I held up a paperback with two lovers in embrace, wind blowing through their ample heads of hair.

It must have seemed like a story out of one of her novels that evening—a woman in her long flowing robe, secretly meeting her lover on the docks in the moonlight. I thought of her socks stuffed into flip-flops and had to chuckle. A professional matchmaker couldn't have come up with a better love connection than her and

Lester. I imaged them holding hands, her with her headlamp and him with his milk jug of urine…

"So who's the third person being blackmailed by Emily?" Harris asked.

I didn't say. I couldn't. At this point it was just a theory, and the last thing in the world I wanted was for Luanne to be a suspect.

"I'm going to find out anyway as soon as we can look at her phone," Harris reminded me.

"Maybe," I said, folding a stack of ratty towels while he watched me. "Do you think Marge could have figured out that Emily and Lester were hooking up? If they got married, she'd have to share a cabin with Emily. I'd kill her myself in that situation."

"According to Lester, he waited each night for Marge to go to sleep, then left the cabin to meet Emily. Plus, if he was awake, there's no way Marge could slip past him. None of the cabins are big enough to slip by someone during their waking hours. Not even theirs. She has an alibi."

"Wait. What? You went without me?" I felt like the youngest child who'd been left behind.

"Sorry. I knocked on your door shortly after lunch, but you didn't answer. I couldn't find you," he said. "It was better that way. I really lost my temper on those two. I'm getting pretty tired of the lies. If I didn't think locking them up would shut 'em up, I'd do it. But the last thing I need is a bunch of lawyers coming around."

"So what happened after Lester went back that night?"

"He said Marge went to bed late that night, so he got to the dock at a quarter past ten. Emily was already dead by then, lying there on the dock. Marge says Lester came into the cabin sobbing and woke her up. She wouldn't let him go for help. Told him it would look like he did it if he went back. She said she was just protecting her brother."

"Poor Lester…that Marge! Maybe Emily might have lived if they had called for help."

"Maybe, although the medical examiner says otherwise—she had a pretty serious brain hemorrhage and probably couldn't have recovered from it anyway. And I'm not sure either Marge or Lester could have pushed her with the force that caused the blow."

"What was their cabin like?" I asked.

"Nice," he said. "You've never seen it?"

"That thing is a fortress. No one goes in. No one really knows what goes on in there. So, nice? How nice? Like granite counters nice?"

"Oh yeah, granite counters, custom cabinetry. Hardwood floors. Great camp style. Rustic, but luxury rustic."

"Oh man. I'd love to see it." Technically, you weren't allowed to alter the structures without permission from Parks, but everyone did it anyway. I'd always fantasized about decorating one of the cabins. It sounded like Marge had done it right. Although I did not care for the lady, she was always dressed impeccably and in good taste. But I imaged things to be too perfect. There was nothing eclectic about Marge Rice.

I saw Jack out of the window and waved for him to come down. He was in his swim shorts and had a couple of towels in his hand.

"I've been looking all over for you. What are you doing in there?" he asked. "I thought you might want to take a swim." He was really trying to please me. We hadn't swum together in ages, and I'd stopped asking.

I pulled him in and shut the door behind him. Jack greeted Harris with a handshake. "We found Emily's phone," I told him.

"*She* found Emily's phone," Harris said.

Jack smiled with what looked like pride.

"Take that swim. I've got this covered," urged Harris.

"Are you sure? You're going to tell me what's on there, right?"
The detective nodded.

"Promise?" I asked.

"Promise," he laughed. "Go! Swim."

"Should I be leaving my wife alone in a cabin with a detective?"
Jack asked on the way down to the swim dock.

"Very funny. I do love this one though. I just love him."

He shook his head and laughed.

The swim dock was bright with primary colors. The sky was a child's blue, reflecting onto the lake. A few billowy clouds were mirrored on the surface. Jacob was sitting under a red umbrella. He gave me a nod, which was as close to a happy greeting as one got from a teenager. Marge Rice was in her usual position in a turquoise canvas beach chair, book in hand, hat covering her ivory skin. Splashes came from Lester as he kicked his way across the swim area. Moe sat resting out on the dock. An emerald ring of trees surrounded the lake, completing what looked like a perfect summer picture.

I pulled my sundress off and jumped off the dock into the water. It was chilly for a moment but felt refreshing and silky once I started moving around. I took deep breaths to catch up from the shock of the cold and shouted to Jack, "It feels great. Just what I needed."

He removed his shirt and prepared for a dive. I watched him while I paddled in place. He'd kept his figure well over the years. Not too buff, but naturally fit. I whistled like a construction worker, and he smiled and dove in. He grabbed my feet underwater. I screamed and kicked and then wrapped myself around him when he came up for air.

We swam out to the dock where Moe was sunbathing. I was still annoyed with him for keeping whatever he knew about Stan from me, so I spun around and swam back toward the main dock. Jack stayed behind and chatted with him while I did some laps. Eventually my husband caught up to me, and we wrestled around some more.

I had my arms around his neck. He was a strong enough swimmer to keep us both afloat.

"Moe can't tell you what happened with Stan because it's board business and he'll get in trouble," he whispered in my ear. "He told me to tell you he's very sorry."

I pulled away and treaded water while I faced him. "The Board had a conversation about a turtle?" I said quietly, not moving my mouth as if there were lip readers everywhere.

He shrugged. "Don't get him in trouble," he said firmly.

"I won't," I whispered back snottily, offended that he thought I would give Moe away.

Marge was watching us with her phony smile. When I got out of the water, I laid my towel down somewhat close so we could chat.

"Can you believe what happened to Stan?" I said to her.

"Who is Stan?" she said, putting down her book to look at me.

"Stan. The turtle that lived here long before we did…?" My sarcasm was coming out. I could not control it on this issue.

"Oh, that horrid beast. Well, better than having him hurt someone." She went back to her book as if it would help to end the conversation.

"Snapping turtles don't hurt people, Marge. Why on earth would you worry about a turtle, anyway? You don't even go in the water." I was holding back my temper with everything I had, but I was starting to boil over.

"Oh, they can be quite vicious—especially on land—and that turtle was getting very used to sunning on this dock."

I looked at Jacob.

"I thought Stan was cool," he shrugged.

"Oh really, so you weren't worried he was going to bite your fucking leg off?" I got louder as the question neared its end. I couldn't help myself and stood up.

"Honey!" Jack whispered. He was standing close by, drying his hair with a towel.

I leaned over Marge's chair and spoke into her face. "If I find out you had anything to do with his death, you are going to answer for it, Marge." She stared up at me like a scared rabbit. I lowered my voice. "I will make sure you answer for it," I whispered into her wide eyes. I picked up my towel and walked up the stairs, leaving her with her mouth agape.

Jack caught up to me. "Are you all right?"

"No, I'm not all right. It's all making sense now." I went straight to Luanne's cabin and knocked on the door. When she didn't answer, I knocked again. Now I knew what Lu and Bobby had been fighting about.

"Luanne!" I said loudly.

"All right already!" she answered. "Is there a fire or somethin'? Jesus."

As soon as the door opened, I asked, "You and Bobby were fighting about Stan, weren't you? Bobby killed Stan, didn't he?"

She didn't answer, instead shaking her head in shame. I headed toward Bobby's cabin, almost running. He came out of the outhouses just as I turned to follow the trail.

"Bobby! You killed that turtle, didn't you? You killed Stan! How could you?"

He took a step back, thrown off by my attack. "He was a danger to the kids, Lee. The Board was worried he'd take someone's toe off," he said defensively.

I lunged forward, completely blind with anger. Jack pulled me back and stepped in between us.

"You are a disgusting person!" I screamed at Bobby. "You are sick! Shame on you! Shame on you!"

Freddie and Detective Harris both came out to see what was going on. Bobby saw them and turned from me. As he walked down the lonely path, his shoulders were slumped and his stance defeated. I went back to my cabin, sat on the sofa, and cried.

Maddy and Roz showed up at my door a few minutes later.

"Did you guys know about this? Tell me the truth," I asked.

"I knew what happened once I heard Stan was dead, but honestly, I had no idea they would do what they did. There was a board meeting last week, and Marge was complaining about the turtle crap on the dock. She asked if Stan could be relocated. 'He's a turtle! He's just gonna swim right back,' I told her," Maddy said.

"Why doesn't *she* relocate?" I asked like I was three years old.

"Bobby kisses her ass. She's been on his side for years so that she can get what she wants done. I never thought he'd do anything like that, though. He's lost his mind," Roz said. "I would have called Parks on him right away, but I was worried about the camp. What if they took our lease? And Luanne begged us not to. She was worried about how it would make us look."

"So you don't want me to go to Parks?" They were silent. I was incredulous.

"It's your choice," Jack said when I looked at him. "You have to follow your conscience."

"What about your conscience?" I said.

"I'm leaving this one to you," he answered.

I resented that. Why wasn't he as angry as I was? "Harris knows. It's probably too late anyway," I said. "What the hell is going on in this place? Do you guys know who killed Emily too?"

The room went silent.

"Oh, you guys. This is getting weird," I said.

"Look, I have my suspicions," Maddy said, "but I have no proof. I haven't talked to anyone about my idea except my husband."

I looked to Roz.

"Ditto." She shrugged her shoulders and left the cabin.

"Come on. Let's go sit on the docks and get high," Maddy whispered in case Roz could hear us.

I looked at Jack, and he waved me on. I was in such a foul mood. He was probably happy to see me go.

"How about a walk instead?" I said. "Let's get Lu."

We had to drag Luanne out of her cabin. The three of us talked about the events of the day briefly and then settled into a weird silence.

"Let's go to Otter Pond," I suggested.

The afternoon light was beginning to fade, and the dense forest provided shade from the setting sun. As we walked up over the narrow camp road, I caught a vision of something black dashing by. I stopped suddenly, as did Luanne and Maddy. About a hundred yards ahead of us, a brown bear ran across the path, scooting three tiny cubs in front of her. Their little downy bodies turned back and forth—their back legs weren't getting along with their front legs yet. One climbed four feet up a tree and stopped, like someone had pinched it and stuck it on the trunk. The whole family froze in place, as did we. I whispered, "Hi, mama." She made eye contact for a second and then dashed up the hill with her three fluffy balls. They disappeared over the rocky hillside.

"Did that just happen?" Maddy asked.

"That was a gift," I said.

"I think I crapped my pants," Luanne said, terror winning over beauty.

We walked on until the road turned into a path along the shoreline of the lake and over the main highway to Otter Pond, then through a grassy meadow. A small stream trickled along the path beside us until we reached the pond. The water was shallow at the edges and covered in lily pads. A chorus of frogs paused as we walked by and continued singing once we moved past them.

At the end of the pond, which was someone's property before the Parks took over, sat the ruins of an old house, long burnt to the ground. A small boathouse survived at the water's edge. We walked through the tall grass to the rotting steps and entered the structure, which was open to the water. I sat down and crossed my legs, facing the pond with a western view. The sun was saying its goodbyes, leaving deep pinks and oranges in the sky and turning the mountains into black silhouettes once again. The pond was still except for the occasional splash of a frog.

A large granite rock served as foundation for one corner of the boathouse. Maddy kicked her flip-flops off and scooted close enough to keep her bottom dry, dipping her feet into the water, which was crystalline over the gray granite. Luanne paced back and forth behind me.

"Luanne, Bobby implied that Emily had something on you. I haven't repeated that to anyone, including Harris, I promise. But I found Emily's phone today. He's going to find out soon enough if she took a video or something." I kept my eyes on the sunset.

"Yeah, she said she had proof. I didn't kill her, though, if that's what you're thinkin'," Luanne insisted.

"I never thought you did, Lu, but if you don't come forward, it'll look bad."

She sighed deeply and explained, "Patrick was taking the day use fees out of the box. I didn't know it! I just thought people weren't payin'. You know how people are. I kept sayin', 'Hey, did you pay your visitors fees?' and people were all defensive with me. Turns out my rotten husband was pillagin' from the camp. He was takin' my keys and openin' the box and stealin' the money. I am such a dummy.

I couldn't believe it when I found out." She wiped a tear from her eye and changed her stance to one of anger. "I am such an idiot," she said in resignation. She sat down next to me and pulled her knees up to her chest.

"For wanting to believe in your husband? That makes you devoted, not stupid," Maddy said.

"Emily figured it out before I did." She chuckled sarcastically while shaking her head. "He was throwin' away the forms. She was pickin' 'em back outta the garbage like a rat. I told her, 'Give 'em to me, and I'll total 'em up and pay the camp back. You'll never see him here again.' But no, she said wanted something from me. She told me to make sure she got a cabin. I told her, 'I don't have nothing to do with it. It's all the Board.' But she just said, 'You can do it.' And then she smiled that cunning smile. She was an evil one that one. A real witch."

"Evil enough to kill?" I asked, not believing for one second that Luanne had been the one to push Emily.

"Hell no, I don't have time for that. I got kids. Who do you think's gonna raise 'em, Patrick?"

"They are old enough to raise themselves now, Lu. It's time to start thinking about yourself," Maddy said.

I knew Luanne was telling the truth. It might be hard to convince Harris of it, though. The sun had set behind the mountains without any compliments from us that evening, but it had been a sadly beautiful show.

It was dark when we got back to camp. I was freaking out the whole way back, thinking we were going to have a run-in with mama bear and get mauled.

"Let's go to the Road House tonight," I said when we were close to camp. I couldn't face another evening in the pavilion. "Let's go drink too much and dance like we're the girlfriends in a motorcycle gang."

"I'm in. I don't feel like cookin' anyway," Luanne agreed.

My husband was on Maddy and Henry's porch. Their cabin was close to the camp entrance and far from the action, the way they liked it. We all agreed that a night at the Road House was much needed and set a meeting time.

I popped in to see Harris before I went back to my cabin. "What'd you find out?" I asked.

"Password protected," he responded.

Good, I thought. That gave me more time to clear Luanne.

CHAPTER 30

A LANTERN HUMMED AND GLOWED, and the sound of shuffling cards harmonized with the crickets. Roz and Jacob were sitting at the picnic table on the patio outside of her cabin. Jacob was the age when many teens started dating and driving and their friends became more important than the lake. Soon he'd have a girlfriend and stop coming up with his parents. Roz and Moe would be heartbroken once more.

"What are you playing?" I asked, walking toward them.

"Gin rummy, want in?" Roz asked.

"Nah. Thanks, though. We're heading down to the Road House for dinner. I need a break from this place."

"I still can't believe Bobby killed Stan. That turtle was cool as hell. He'd never hurt anybody. He hissed at me once, but if you left him alone, he left you alone," Jacob said.

"We're all responsible. I should have shut Marge down at the meeting," Roz said. "I don't know who that woman thinks she is."

"I hope we get her cabin," Jacob said.

"So do I," I said.

He gave me a half smile. "Yeah, but we're only taking the cabin if it's the Rices'. Dad wouldn't do that to Therese or Roz and Moe," he said.

"What are you talking about? That's not how it works. Fair is fair. That's what a lottery is," Roz said. If she'd heard this from Jacob before, she was a good pretender. "All this talk about politics is garbage. The lottery was created to keep things fair, and that's how it's going to go. You do your work, you get in the lottery. That simple."

Roz certainly did her fair share around the camp, as did Therese. They were an integral part of what made the camp special. Roz managed cabin rentals and taught wildlife and nature classes. Moe served on the board of directors and organized cleanup days. Therese ran the swim docks and managed the lifeguards. These people were institutions here. Emily had been a threat to them all.

"Yeah, well, I like the cabin we're in now anyway. It's the best cabin," Jacob said.

The Road House was filled with regulars: the retired fireman whose wife had left him, the soft-hearted biker with his whiskey-stained beard, the middle-aged divorcee in too-tight clothes, the uninspired artist, the journeyman electrician, the rich man from Tuxedo Park who hated his wife, the lonely, the bored, the ravenous. They were all here, drinking to find laughter and companionship and maybe a soft touch for just one night.

I was drinking to forget. A local band blasted a blues song. I hated blues—all of the songs sounded the same to me—but tonight it seemed fitting. I ordered bourbon neat and a Guinness and reminded Jack that he was designated driver.

The Road House bar was rectangular in shape with an A-line ceiling that sported an enormous moose head along with a set of mounted bull horns, a deer head, a neon beer sign, a tin iron workers' union logo, and other found or donated memorabilia. A narrow aisle surrounded the bar, which forced you to get to know your neighbors, like it, or not.

When I looked around, I saw a few more familiar faces, including Officer Lars Carter. I had forgotten that he lived close by. Since Harris was in camp, I figured it must be Carter's night off. He was wearing a plaid shirt and was hovering over his beer. I threw him a nod and he returned it.

I also spotted Tom Johnson as he headed out the back entrance. I scooted and twisted through the crowd to get to the door. I was grateful for the fresh cool air and lack of music when I popped out of the hot room and onto the deck.

He was smoking a cigarette and looking over the railing to the creek.

"We meet again," I said.

"Oh, hey, Lee," he said, turning momentarily.

Part of Tom Johnson's appeal had always been his large frame. He was probably six foot four—the kind of guy who could carry a tall woman like me—a man I could look up to. Defeat could shrink you, though, and tonight he seemed somehow smaller. His grayed T-shirt and faded jeans hung loosely, and he looked like his camp—in need of some maintenance. His leathery face screamed, "no more sun." I vowed to wear a hat on the lake tomorrow.

I stood beside him, leaning on the railing. "How are things going over there?" I asked.

He chuckled with resignation, like it couldn't really get worse. "Nineteen more days with the ladies from hell," he said. "I used to be a Christian till I met them. My wife's leaving me. I'm handing the camp back to Parks. I have no education, no money, and no job."

"You have love," I reminded him.

He looked at me like it was the first time he'd really seen me and then returned his eyes to the creek below us. "No secrets on the lake I guess."

"No secrets," I confirmed.

"I do love her. I've loved her for a long time."

There it was again, that excitement for the two of them. It felt so romantic to me. I'd know Therese for eight years but had never seen her with a partner. Luanne had told me that she was divorced a long time ago. Even though she didn't have kids of her own, she was so incredibly generous with everyone else's. All of us owed her a lot. She deserved to be happy.

"Life is incredibly short, Tom. Live it while you can."

He chuckled again.

"Did you see her down there that night?" I asked. "Did you see Emily laying there?"

He was quiet for a moment, which gave me my answer. "Terrie walked me down to the dock after my visit. We saw her there, but if we had said anything, we'd have to admit we were seeing each other, and I thought we weren't ready. She looked pretty dead, and honestly, Terrie's been a mess about it. She's been protecting my marriage... after everything I've put her through, making her wait..."

"Did she step in blood that night?"

"No. No way! I park my boat in the bushes. We didn't even walk on the actual dock, only the ramp."

Yet somebody had wanted it to look like Therese was there.

"I see better days for you two, Tom," I said, patting him on the shoulder.

"I never saw myself as a cheat. Joan and I haven't had a good marriage for at least ten years. We stuck it out for the kids, but we both knew we got married for the wrong reasons. I figured the kids would be off on their own soon and it would be simpler that way. I'm not waiting anymore. We're not waiting any more."

Maddy came through the doors from the bar, and for a moment, the sound of blues guitar filled the deck. "There you are! Look what I've got." She held up a joint. "Hey, Tom."

"Hey, Maddy."

"You want?" she said, lighting up.

"Why not?" Tom said, smiling.

The three of us stood on the deck, smoking our way into a peaceful moment. It's true that hippies have no rhythm. We spent the rest of the night dancing in laughter to what sounded like one long song.

CHAPTER 31

CLOUDS SAT LIKE TIRED TRAVELERS on the ridge of the mountains and provided the perfect resting place until the sun warmed up and scared them off to mysterious places. My head was not so lucky. The fog of abuse from the night before hung low in my brain and weighed on my eyelids.

It always seemed like a good idea to party it up while I was doing it, but I found myself questioning my own behavior again and again and made promises to my body that it knew I would not keep.

I attempted to do some yoga on the dock, but every time I bent over, it hurt my brain, which felt like a dehydrated walnut rattling around in my cranium. Instead I sat on a towel with my legs crossed and smoked some weed—the cheater's way to a meditative state.

My mind kept going back to the blood on the dock behind me. It was gone, but somehow it lingered over the area like a bad spirit. For a moment I resented Emily, but then I remembered her mission that night and gave her grace. It wasn't like she'd meant to bleed all over my place of Zen.

I took deep breaths to get centered. *It has washed away. It has washed away.* This would be my new mantra while I was on the dock with the birds and the frogs and the fish, all of whom faced death every day and yet still flew the same skies and croaked their songs and lived in the same waters where turtles fed on them and fishermen made them dinner. Today I would celebrate the fact that I was alive.

Roz came down with her boat, quietly, like her beaver spirit animal. She was all geared up in her fishing vest and shorts. She hopped in her little green canoe and paddled away with only a "Hello," respecting the code of the morning hour.

Soon after Roz had drifted away, Delia came out and laid her towel down on the dock below her cabin. She waved when she saw me. I waved back, and she picked up her things and disappeared. To my dismay, she next materialized on my dock.

"Good morning!" she chimed like a happy songbird.

She had tiny pedal-pusher-length yoga pants on with a bright pink racerback tank top. Her chestnut curls were in a high pompom on her head. The perkiness of her demeanor made my head throb.

"Morning," I whispered.

"Want to do some yoga?" she asked. "I just took a power yoga course and learned some amazing new poses."

I hate doing yoga with others. I'm not comfortable with my butt in the air, and I feel fat and weak when skinny people like Delia can hold a pose without their bodies vibrating in pain.

"Nah, I'm a little under the weather this morning," I replied.

"Oh, so sorry to hear that. Yoga might be just what you need."

"I'm good," I said. "Where's Randy?" I asked. I didn't really care where he was, but I wanted to make sure he wasn't going to show up too.

"He's still asleep. He and Jacob did a night paddle. They were up late for the meteor shower. Did you see it?"

"No, I was boozing it up at Earl's," I confessed. "Do they go out night paddling a lot?"

"Mostly just Jacob, but sometimes Randy too."

I wondered where Jacob was the night of Emily's death and reminded myself to ask Harris when I saw him. If I asked Delia, her cheery demeanor would flee the dock like a flock of scared birds.

"You don't worry about him on the lake by himself?" I asked.

"We had to stop worrying, Lee, because he does whatever he wants anyway. What can we do? He's not a bad kid. He really isn't."

"I've gotten to know him a little better this week. He's a good guy," I said with sincerity.

She smiled the way a mother does when you compliment her child. I realized for the first time that she *was* his mother. Maybe she hadn't delivered him, but she was doing all of the hard work.

The conversation made me miss my own boys. There was a permanent ache when they weren't with me, but it didn't serve a purpose other than to hurt, so I stuffed it down. Today was the first day we were allowed to call them at camp, so I was thinking of them even more than I usually did.

It was time to go see if Harris was up yet. I took my coffee mug and towel and left Delia on my dock to stretch her skinny limbs.

The detective was in the great room, talking on the phone. He was wearing a polo shirt with a park emblem and khakis. His feet were up on the folding table, and he was leaning back in the chair while he held the phone to his ear. He motioned for me to sit, but I was feeling restless.

The walls held onto the smoke from a hundred years of campfires, and I breathed it in. I walked around touching the blackened surfaces of the trophy cups on the mantle. If they'd been found at a flea market, they would have sold in seconds. Yet there they were, hard won by past club members, invisible to the present. I picked up the warped one and found an old button and some dust hiding inside. I thought of buying silver polish the next time I went into town but knew they would go home in someone's bag if they shined too brightly.

I'd heard enough of Harris's conversation to know he was discussing the flip-flops with someone.

"Well, it was Emily's blood for sure, but there were no prints, nothing. They were wiped clean," he told me when he hung up.

"Where's her phone?" I asked.

"Right here. You want to help me guess her password?" he pulled it out of his shirt pocket.

"Hmm…Did you try four-three-two-one?"

He nodded.

"Six-six-six?" I laughed.

He tried it even though I wasn't serious.

"What did Emily love? That's a tough one. Pain. Suffering. Complaining. Rules. What numeric sequence would she get excited about? I'm going to have to think about this. Can't you send it out to someone to crack? Call the phone company or something?"

"I'm working on it, but they want a warrant. It's going to take some time," he explained.

"I'll keep thinking. Maybe go through her stuff again. Would you mind?"

"Please, I'd be grateful." He smiled.

"Hey, where did Jacob Foster say he was the night of Emily's death?"

"Jacob, let's see…" He shuffled around the desk until he found a file and pulled out a sheet of paper with Jacob's statement.

"In his cabin all night. Didn't feel well."

"So no alibi," I said. "Randy and Delia were with me at Johnson Beach. Did anyone see him?"

He shook his head.

"What are you thinking?"

"Well, he's quite loyal to Therese and also to Roz and Moe. They've been his family all of these years. Especially Roz. Tom told me they saw Emily lying on the docks but couldn't say anything because of their affair, and I believe him."

"Did he now?" His look was more perturbed than surprised. "Well that's interesting because it isn't what he told me." He looked about as angry as he was capable of looking.

"But you can understand why, right? There's a lot at stake for them."

He rolled is eyes. "No I can't, Lee! They lied to me. There are a bunch of liars in this camp." His face was red, and I backed up a little.

"I know. It's understandable that you're angry, but they were protecting their secret...and Tom's family. I saw him at the Road House last night. He feels terrible about it. He asked Therese not to come forward until he spoke to his wife."

"I don't mean to shoot the messenger, Lee, but what else are you people hiding?"

I didn't say a word.

He took a deep breath to regain his composure and tried to be nice. "So if they are telling the truth now, we're narrowing down opportunity to Roz and Moe, Marge, Lester, Jacob, Bobby...and Luanne." He looked me in the eyes to see my response to this last name as he spoke it.

"Yes, that would be the list. But Moe and Roz have each other as alibis," I said, not giving him what he wanted, which was a response to his mention of Luanne. "Hey, what date is Emily's birthday?"

He shuffled through the paperwork like it was a pile of autumn leaves and pulled out a piece of paper. "April fifteenth. I tried it," he said, referring to the code for her phone. "I tried the year also. She turned seventy in April."

"Try the year backwards."

He punched in the numbers. "Nope."

I had one last thought. "Let me," I said, holding out my hand. I typed in 3-6-6-8. "Yes!" I yelled. "The password is D-O-N-T. Don't. Jeez, Emily," I mumbled, shaking my head. I handed the phone back to Harris, excited and worried about what he would find.

CHAPTER 32

As we scrolled through her photos, it occurred to me that Emily had fancied herself a naturalist, taking blurry close up shots of berries and leaves, a portrait of a shiny beetle, and an uncentered group of ants eating a dead fly. There was a selfie of her wearing bright pink sunglasses that had a doctor's name printed in white down one arm and her worn Hawaiian shirt hanging from her bony shoulders. I could see the lake in the background through the trees. She looked exactly as if she was about to lecture someone about rules and dangers, or about her aches and pains. Or maybe she was about to gloat about how she knew things, hidden things that people stored away like squirrels store nuts for the winter.

After staring at the self-portrait for several moments, I swiped past it, and a completely different face appeared. It had the same wild gray hair and tired clothing, only this woman was smiling. Her worn teeth were exposed, and her eyes were kind and vulnerable. I realized that I'd never seen Emily smile in the brief time I'd known her. I wondered which photo was the real Emily.

There were other photos: a license plate number and a blurry photo of a "No Parking" sign, buildings, a squirrel, some birds in Central Park...there was even one of me swimming off of the rock.

"Bitch," I mumbled.

"So you're the other person she was blackmailing?" Harris said, laughing.

"I have an alibi, remember?" I said.

Eventually came a series of photos of Tom and Therese locked in an embrace. They were standing on the rock, the same one where I originally met Emily. She must have run into them while hiking. The last item on the phone was a video of Bobby mixing concrete and shoveling it into wooden forms on the stairs down to the pool. Emily had provided a voice over, which included sarcastic comments about Bobby's disability.

I was relieved. There was nothing about Luanne. I left the pavilion so I could let her know. The fear would be eating her up by now.

Luanne was reading a paperback, her thick-rimmed glasses sitting halfway down her nose. She looked up at me when she heard footsteps.

"Sidown," she said to me.

"I get to call my kids today, Lu. Any chance I could do it from your cabin?"

"Of course. What time?"

"Noon."

"No problem. I got a chimney guy comin' today to check the fireplace in the pavilion. I don't like all the sparks comin' out onto the roof like that."

"Thanks," I said. "Hey, Harris got into Emily's phone. There's nothing on it. No photos of anything relating to you."

Her eyes welled up, and she wiped a tear that attempted to roll down her cheek. "This has been a nightmare." She sighed. "I haven't slept in days."

"I know, Lu," I said sympathetically. "She did have a photo of me swimming in the lake that day," I added to change the subject.

"Jesus H. Christ. She was beggin' to be killed."

We both laughed, but something was wrong. There was a tension between us.

"Have you seen Bobby?" I asked.

"Not since you scared the crap out of him yesterday. He's probably hidin' in shame."

"As he should be," I said, enraged anew at the thought of what he had done. "He can't undo what he did. If he's capable of strangling an innocent animal, what else is he capable of?"

"You think he killed Emily?" she asked. "Nah, no way. He's an idiot, don't get me wrong, but I can't see it."

"He killed a turtle, Lu. For sunning on the swim dock," I reminded her. "As far as I'm concerned, the guy is capable of anything."

I was so excited about talking to my kids that I wouldn't take Red out until after the phone call—just in case I got stranded somewhere and missed my noon appointment with them. Jack and I entered Luanne's cabin five minutes before noon. I spoke to them first, pretending not to miss them as much as I did so they wouldn't get homesick. They were having a great time and filled my ears with tales of summer adventures. Max had gotten into some trouble for wandering off alone, which was no surprise. He was just like his mother; structure was the enemy.

While Jack took his turn speaking to the boys, I wandered around the tiny, clutter-filled space Luanne called home. Her desk was piled high with paperwork. An estimate for a chimney cap sat on the top of the stack. On the bookshelf next to her desk were labeled binders:

Cabin Rentals, Board Meetings, and Day Use Forms. I picked the last binder up and flipped it open on the tabletop. My eyes could not comprehend what they were looking at.

Luanne came into the room and saw me standing over the open book. We stood there staring at each other, neither of us moving. Jack glanced back and forth at us both and wrinkled his brow. "Okay, buddy. Love you too. Talk to you next week."

I had no concept of time. The shock of learning that Luanne had the missing forms sent me reeling. Tears welled in both of our eyes as we continued to look at each other.

"What's wrong?" Jack asked. "What's going on?"

"It was you. You ransacked Emily's cabin," I whispered.

"I begged her to give me the forms. I had the money! No harm done. I begged her. The cabins were outta my hands." She wiped her eyes and took a deep breath.

"Oh, Lu." I couldn't say another word. Tears were streaming down my face too, but I couldn't move to wipe them.

"I didn't kill her. I swear on my mother's grave. I didn't kill her."

The book lay open, and inside was a stack of forms, different from the rest by their deep crease down the center from a previous fold. A few had stains, like they'd been in the trash. Others were torn along the edges.

"After you guys left, I was heading back to my cabin when I saw Emily in her ratty old robe, walking down to the dock. Since I knew she'd be gone, I went to her cabin to look for the papers. I figured they had to be in there somewhere. I found some gloves under the sink and put 'em on. I knew she would call the police in the morning, so I figured I'd cover my ass. The more I looked, the angrier I got. Pretty soon I was flippin' things over and tossin' them around. I didn't care anymore. I was so mad at Patrick for getting me into this mess and for Emily for making a bad situation worse. I didn't wanna lose my job. I love this place. It's the only break I get, comin' up here." She continued to swipe at tears.

"So where were they?" I asked.

"She had 'em taped underneath her kitchen table. Figures. She complained earlier in the season that there was gum under there and made me scrape it off."

I gave myself a mental slap for not looking under there, though what would I have seen? Maybe tape marks at least.

"Then I brought the papers here and put them back in the book. I spent all night figuring out what I was going to say to the Board when the extra money showed up. I didn't sleep a wink. When I found her on the dock, I was scared outta my mind. I knew it would look bad for me. That's why I didn't tell anyone what I did."

Poor Luanne. All of her rules were broken in one night. She'd turned a blind eye to our pranks at Johnson Camp, she'd entered someone else's cabin without consent, and she'd taken something from it. And then she lied to cover her tracks. It was too much for a woman like her to bear.

"This story does not leave this cabin," I finally ordered.

CHAPTER 33

THE ROAD THAT SNAKED THROUGH Harriman State Park was named Seven Lakes Drive for a reason. The gentle curves of the two-lane passage was thick with lush summer forest and provide the rider with awe by exposing each mountain lake by skirting their unique shorelines; one was rocky with islands speckled with blueberry shrubs and determined evergreens; another had soft edges and a solitary fisherman on its shoreline.

"God, I love this road." I whispered out the window, which was open and blowing my hair around into what would be impossible tangles. I didn't care. It felt like freedom. I pulled a strand out of my mouth. "We have to remember to come up this winter," I said louder, so Jack could hear. The road was spectacular in any season, but the ice and snow provided the park with a winter dazzle that was breathtaking. When the lakes froze over, ice fishermen would dot the surface with their poles and folding chairs and soup-filled thermoses.

At the top of the hill, a traffic circle with a stone ranger's station in its center overlooked the largest and most crowded lake, the only public swimming beach in the park. The primary colors from beach balls and swimmer's suits contrasted against the natural backdrop of stone and woods and water. The faint smell of sunblock filled the air for just a moment.

I'd asked Jack to get me out of Camp Death for a while. We were headed to Bear Mountain, which was a spectacular twenty-minute drive up the park road. The occasional rustic stone outbuilding nestled into the woods, long past their use and now part of the forest. The park had an old-timey cartoon feel, like your picnic basket would be snatched by talking bears in bow ties if left unattended.

"Luanne didn't kill Emily," I said out loud, like that would make it true.

"I know," Jack responded.

"How do you know?" I looked at him while he drove.

"Because I don't believe she has it in her to hide the truth."

"But she hid the forms…"

"Not really. She put them in the book. And she told you about them, right? That's not exactly hiding the truth."

I grinned at the thought of Luanne turning Emily's cabin upside down. She really must have lost it to behave like that. "Poor thing," I said quietly.

The Bear Mountain Inn's facade was what all mountain lodges should aspire to be: boulders and timber rising together to create a building that complimented the rugged mountain that ascended behind it. Bob Dylan and Joni Mitchell had both written songs behind its walls. The Inn had been undergoing renovations the entire time we'd been coming up here. During each visit I would press my face against its enormous old leaded windows to catch a glimpse inside. I couldn't wait to get inside one day.

Behind the Inn sat Hessian Lake, a granite bowl filled with pure spring water. It was said that the lake was on a fault line, which is why the waters were so clean. It's constantly spring fed and always draining through the abyss, and in the heat, it was almost impossible not to want to dive in despite the "No Swimming" signs clearly posted as we followed the walking path around its shores. I wasn't one to follow the rules, especially when no one was looking, but I wouldn't put my baby toe in that lake. Someone drowned in Hessian Lake almost yearly.

Back in 1777, a bloody Revolutionary War battle took place on the lake's shores, then called Highland Lake. Tory and Hessian soldiers marched through Doodletown—the ruins of which were now part of the park—and a battle ensued. The settlers got the best of them, and the bodies of more than two hundred and fifty Hessian soldiers were thrown into the lake. Witnesses said the crystalline waters turned blood red for days. The lake was called Bloody Pond until the Parks renamed it Hessian Lake in 1915. It was said that ghosts of the mercenaries lived in the water and pulled people under.

I peered into the clear waters looking for signs of centuries old remains. All I spotted was a red solo cup and a plastic water bottle. "Fucking plastic waste," I mumbled.

Jack had been listening to my rants on this subject for many years. He kicked off his sneakers and stepped into the water, grabbing the items. He was wearing a soft cotton V-neck T-shirt with army green shorts that looked like they just came off the rack. I looked down at my wrinkled cotton tank dress and noticed a small hole by the hem. My hair was lumpy with tangles. I smoothed it back a bit and tied it into a high bun.

"I'm not getting every item we see," he warned me with a grumpy look.

"Thank you." I smiled, nuzzling against him. Things felt fresh between us, like we were new lovers.

The trail parted ways with the shoreline as we headed uphill. I looked down at the waters, wondering what it must have been like to see them after the battle, crimson with death.

"Of all the places to go today, you had to pick this one." Jack laughed.

"I love this place. Despite its gruesome history, you have to admit it's beautiful. Its real name is Sinnipink Lake. That's what the Native Americans called it. Why do the Hessians get the name?" I wondered out loud.

"Yeah, well they can change the name, but it's always going to be Bloody Pond to me," he said.

"I hope Emily's death doesn't define our lake," I said.

"You mean Emily's murder?" he reminded me.

"Was it murder? I mean, it could've been more like a crime of passion. But who is that passionate? I don't see Bobby behaving like that. He's so…"

"Doped up."

"Yeah, doped up."

It was time to think of something besides camp. We hit the trail to Doodletown, which was a steep uphill climb and involved a river of ankle-twisting boulders as a path. When the English marched through Doodletown, the residents mocked them. It was the only way they could protest. They say the song "Yankee Doodle Came to Town," was written about the battle. I had it in my head that day as we walked the path along the shoreline.

When we finally arrived, I sat on the edge of a stone foundation to rest. I thought I'd die from exhaustion. "Do you think in two hundred years people will walk through the ruins of our neighborhood?" I asked.

He was pacing in front of me to cool down.

"It's a strange thought. Nothing is really permanent is it?"

When the New York State Park system took the land, the remaining residents refused to leave. It wasn't until the 1960s that the last holdout died.

"Can you imagine getting up here with supplies? I barely dragged my own body up that hill," I said, red faced and still sweating from the hike up.

I thought about my own emotional struggles and felt like a fool. My internal battles were nothing compared to the physical challenges these people had endured. They'd left their families and sailed to a new land, hiked up a hill, endured the harsh winters, and built a settlement, then watched it threatened by a brutal war. What would they think of me, a spoiled stoner with a life of luxury who constantly questioned her happiness? I vowed to remember them the next time I felt sorry for myself.

As we walked back down the trail, which once served as a road, we passed two little lakes, one with a waterfall dropping into it. The lushness of the forest created a lacy border around a pond, which felt storybook-like in its perfection. Nearby, a small sign indicated the foundation of an old schoolhouse. People here must've lived lives of "quiet isolation," as Thoreau would say.

We crossed the Hudson River over the Bear Mountain Bridge and headed north to dine in one of the many towns that graced the historic river. After dinner we watched the sunset from a gazebo on the embankment. I tried to be present. It was a gorgeous summer night, and the cliffs across the water were filled with the old stone castles of West Point Academy, a perfect marriage of history and beauty.

But all I could think about was camp.

"Come on, let's go," Jack said, sensing my anxiety.

"Sorry, hon. There's something nagging me. Something I can't put my finger on. I really want to go back to figure it out," I said.

"I know," he said, holding my hand as we walked to the car. "I've known all day."

The camp road was black with night, but several cabin lights glowed amber, and the aura of flames filled the pavilion with firelight.

Embers made their way up the chimney and died in the space over the building. I wondered if Luanne was stressing out about it somewhere. Campfires were considered community events, so we walked up to see who had started the blaze. Roz and Moe were sitting in front of the large crackling fire. Detective Harris was there too, sitting in an Adirondack chair, beer in hand, enjoying the blaze.

"Well look at you!" I said, honestly surprised.

He looked comfortable in a zip-up sweatshirt and jeans, like one of the campers.

"Carter had a date tonight, so I'm sleeping here with you folks." He smiled.

I thought for a second about what kind of woman would go out with Carter. I could not materialize an image. "We still need babysitting?" I asked.

"It's not exactly torture to hang around. You guys have a little bit of paradise here. I may become a member if you'll let me in," he said.

Emily's death had distracted me from the lake's beauty. Getting away had given me a fresh appreciation of it. I filled them in on our adventure and listened patiently as Moe told the story of Hessian Lake once again. This time he added helmeted ghosts and stories of screams in the night.

"What's going to happen to Emily's body?" I asked Harris.

"That's a good question. I spoke to her landlord today. She didn't have any friends or family that can be found. She'll most likely end up on Hart Island."

"Where is that?" I asked.

"It's next to City Island in the Bronx," Moe explained. "Ominous place. Littered with the ruins of an old prison. Lots of mass graves. Babies and homeless and prisoners I think."

I shuddered. Even though I don't believe in an afterlife of any kind, there was still something so depressing about someone's final resting place being in a potter's field.

"That's right. It's the largest mass grave in the United States," Harris added.

"Why don't they just cremate her? Take up less space?" I asked.

"They don't cremate unclaimed bodies. Just in case someone shows up and wants them. It happens," Moe said in response to the incredulous face I made. "During the eighties, the morgues couldn't keep up with all of the AIDs deaths. Young people were dying faster than families could be located. Many sad parents found their kids buried on Hart Island."

We all sat in silence, the glow of the fire exposing our somber faces.

"Do you paddle, Jed?" asked Roz, changing the subject. She had a stick in the fire with a marshmallow on it.

"Well, if you call a rowboat paddling, then yes. I take my fishing boat out on Lake Tiorati sometimes. Other than that, the only time I'm on the water is when there's ice fishing." He laughed. "I like that little canoe of yours though. I wouldn't mind getting one of those maybe."

"You can't. I built it myself, twenty years ago. They don't sell the kits anymore," Roz replied with pride.

"It's the envy of the lake," I said. "I looked everywhere for a canoe that light with that much space."

"The Old Town Pack Canoe is a good choice. Thirty-three pounds. Nice space. Gets you out of the water," Roz commented.

Roz knew everything. She knew everything, she saw everything, and normally she heard everything. Harris was watching me. It occurred to me that he wasn't really here because Carter had a date. He was such a wise little detective.

CHAPTER 34

"WHEN WAS THE LAST TIME you saw Bobby?" I asked Roz, Maddy, and then finally Luanne again the next morning.

"I'm sure he's fine," she said. "He's just hiding in shame."

"Just humor me and go check on him please."

His van hadn't moved in two days.

"All right. All right. I'm goin'."

I followed her down the path, trailing behind her both because she speed walked everywhere and because I wasn't in a hurry to actually see Bobby, just to know that he was okay. I stood back on the path and waited while she knocked. Luanne opened the door and disappeared. She started to shout for me.

I ran to the door to see what was wrong. She was in Bobby's room, where he was lying on his bed, gray and bloated, in the same clothes he was wearing the last time I saw him. There was a prescription bottle next to the bed. It smelled like he had been there for days. "Is he alive?" I asked, sure the answer would be no. Vomit was stuck on his face and his pillow.

"He's breathin'. Go to my cabin and call 911. Go!"

I ran back to the great room, where Harris was, and he called it in. He rushed back out to Bobby's cabin but asked me to stand on the road so that emergency services would know how to get to him. It took what felt like a very long time before the paramedics arrived. Bobby was a big man, and the paramedics struggled to carry him down the stairs of his cabin and over the trail that led to the road, but he was still alive when they rolled him into the back of the ambulance.

Our last meeting played in my mind like a black-and-white movie, which brought to mind Stan and his unjust demise. I'd always really liked Bobby but now could not find any respect for him at all. I hoped he would be well, but that was all I could muster.

Luanne and Harris walked out behind the paramedics looking somber. Therese came up to see what was going on, and Randy followed shortly after. Randy and Bobby were close, and Randy was a mess.

"I should have checked on him. I've been distracted. He's been a mess since…" he looked my direction, and if a scatterbrain like Randy was capable of showing anger, he did.

I kept my mouth shut for once. Thinking back, I hadn't seen much of Randy or Bobby in days. Usually they could be found tinkering with some project or another around camp. Neither of them were big paddlers. I doubted Bobby had stepped foot on a boat in years. Since Emily's death, neither of them had been around at all, together or apart.

There was going to be some drama with Randy, and I was going to be the target, so I walked back to my cabin while the others were talking in a group. I was amazed that everyone had forgiven Bobby so many crimes. If he had stolen funds from camp and had defrauded disability, then killed an important protected creature in the park, why was he even allowed in camp at all? This family of friends was all too tolerant, and I was starting to believe someone was protecting a killer.

I was putting the pieces together in my head when I heard my name called. Harris was following me, and we walked toward the dock together.

"Pretty sly maneuver, Detective. Are you really thinking of joining the club?" I said in a low voice, knowing how words traveled in the quiet of the woods.

It was a glorious morning, although with all that had happened, an air of sorrow was hanging over the camp. The lake was as smooth as draped silk, and the clouds were pulled cotton puffs against the periwinkle sky. A fisherman sat peacefully in the quiet of the cove. A white-sailed Sunfish sat in lifeless disappointment across the lake since the wind had plans elsewhere. I could see tiny kayakers far off and wondered if they were Jack and Henry.

"You all have a little piece of heaven here. A coveted paradise," he repeated, not answering my question.

"Coveted. Yes. Interesting choice of words. Do you think Bobby will make it?" I asked.

"Looks like a suicide attempt, and who knows how long he was there?" He shook his head and shrugged. "Time will give us the answer."

"I feel guilty for not feeling guilty," I confessed.

"There you go, telling the truth again," he chuckled.

"Do you think he killed Emily? I mean he had both motive and opportunity. And now we know he's capable," I reminded him. I wanted it to be Bobby. If he was the killer, we could wrap this whole thing up neatly and move on.

"Well, if he did, he served up his own justice. But remember, Lee, whoever pushed Emily just left her to die."

"If you're going to arrest someone for that, you'll have to take half the camp away," I reminded him. "Everyone else seems to have his or her own theories. Roz and Maddy both have their suspects, but neither is sharing. Maybe because it wasn't premeditated? Or because Emily was not liked? I don't know…"

"So you're telling me you don't have any idea?" he asked, looking me in the eyes.

"Oh, I have an idea, but no proof. What good is that?"

"You gonna share that idea with me?"

"Can't we just say it was Bobby and move on?" I asked, only partially joking.

The figures from across the lake made their way closer and closer until I could recognize the boats as Jack and Henry's. I was torn between helping my fellow campers and helping Harris do his job.

"I don't know if I can, Jed. I have to really think about it," I said with tears in my eyes. "I'm sorry. Just let me think about it okay?"

He stood up from the chair next to mine and gathered himself, dusting off his trousers and looking out to the lake. He shook his head in disappointment. "No one should be left to die like that."

We were silent for a few moments. Jack and Henry were close enough to hear our voices. "Will you give me some time? I want to talk to Jack, and then I'll come to you?"

"Yeah. Sure," he said, walking away up the path, awash in disappointment.

A push. I'd been guilty of more than one. The last person I'd pushed (besides Bobby) was an unworthy boyfriend from my freshman year in college. *What if Bobby had fallen when I pushed him? Would that have made me a murderer? But then again, what kind of person goes around pushing people?* I felt an upwelling of shame for my childish behavior. Then I remembered Stan.

A fond friendship died with that turtle—a lost innocence in the summer folks. But I wasn't ready to call anyone a murderer. And I did not want to be the person responsible for bringing them to justice. I had lied to Harris just like everyone else had. I didn't need to talk to Jack. There were things I had to do first, so that I could be sure. I was buying time.

Jack and I had lunch on the patio. He grilled some veggies for me, reminding me of the first day that I had arrived, when I thought everyone in camp was made of beautiful dirt and lake and sunshine.

"What's going on with you? You okay?" Jack asked, concerned by my silence.

"I have to do something. Something that's going to be very hard," I told him and then started to cry.

He took my hands and pulled me out of the chair and hugged me. I was so grateful that we had fixed things between us. I don't know what I would have done if I still had the weight of losing my marriage and family on me.

I allowed myself to cry for only a moment before pulling away. "Time to pay the price for sticking my nose where it doesn't belong." I laughed, wiping my tears, and headed up the path to Therese's cabin.

Therese answered the door and greeted me with the same coolness she'd give a Jehovah's Witness.

"Sorry to come without calling first." My joke fell flat.

"Are you all right?" she asked. I must have looked like a mess after crying: red eyes, my ponytail propped back up by pulling it apart, which made a mess in the back of my head.

"I'm okay," I said weakly, taking a deep breath so I wouldn't cry again. "Can I come in?"

She was surprised but opened the door for me. I'd never been in her cabin, but it looked just as I would have expected. The living room and kitchen were open like my cabin, but her furniture had been assembled here in the cabin from a big box store. Everything was light wood and white against the darker, more golden knotty paneling that lined the walls. Her tiny kitchen had white painted cabinetry with the original black iron pulls and handles. The counters were from the 1950s—I could tell by the aluminum rim around the edges. They were a pale blue, as were the linoleum floors. Everything was in its place. Therese motioned for me to sit down on the futon that served as a sofa.

"I have to ask you a question about the night of Emily's murder. I am sure you are aware that whomever took your shoes that night wanted to make sure you were blamed?"

"Yeah, I'm aware. I already told Harris the truth about what happened that night and why I lied originally," she said, crossing her arms. "What's this about?"

"Can you just tell me, did you leave to use the restroom or go anywhere after you saw Emily's body?"

"No. I came right back here. I did go up to the restrooms, but it was before Tom left. Why?"

"Because someone said they heard footsteps that night. It was suggested that it could have been you walking to the restrooms."

She stood up, indignant. "Who the hell is trying to make it look like I did this? Christ, I would think it was Emily, but she's dead!"

"I'm going to let Harris fill you in, okay? It's really not my place."

"What *is* your place anyway?"

"I don't have one," I said and left her cabin to go see Harris.

I told him what I knew and what I suspected, and we devised a plan. Then I walked back to my cabin and stayed there.

CHAPTER 35

My boys were roughhousing, which culminated in testosterone-filled wrestling like it always did. I heard myself say the words—the ones every mother says at least a hundred times: "Someone is going to get hurt." They ignored me, grabbing and slapping and swatting at each other. We were at the edge of the Grand Canyon.

"Look, you guys! One of the most beautiful things you will ever see."

We were standing behind the railing at first, looking down at the sunset rainbow of earthen walls. Suddenly, the railing disappeared. I could feel the fear, my own fear of heights, an energy that traveled down my arms and feet fast, causing me to tremble.

"Knock it off!" I yelled, but it was too late. My boys tumbled over the edge into the chasm.

I let out a guttural scream and sat up. The alpine pattern of the bedroom curtains assured me that I was okay. It had been just a dream. It was hot, but a breeze was coming off the lake, and the fabric on the windows ballooned from the air. I opened them to see the daylight fading. My nap was over, and it was time to go.

Jack had gone to town to get some work done in the tiny local library, which used to be a chapel but now offered free internet and space for book clubs and after-school tutoring. He hadn't been here when Emily was murdered, and it seemed appropriate that he would miss the meeting Harris had called for five o'clock that evening.

The detective had sent Carter around to each cabin to let all the other campers know that their presence was mandatory. I arrived first and took a seat at one of the chairs that was set up in a half circle. I waited by myself. I felt nervous, like I was about to attend my first AA meeting—which who knows, maybe I would some day. I tapped my hand on the chair next to me and fidgeted around in my seat.

Marge and Lester showed up next, but I had nothing to say to Marge and hoped Luanne and Maddy would get here soon. Roz and Moe were next to arrive, and Roz struck up a conversation with Marge and Lester—something about the Cabin Committee and a new refrigerator for one of the kitchens. Maddy and Henry came in and took a seat next to me.

"What do you think the police want?" Henry whispered.

I shrugged as if I were in the dark.

Freddie showed up and leaned against the railing, away from the chairs. Everyone greeted him as if he were just arriving to camp, mostly to break the uncomfortable silence. He was dressed in a flannel shirt and thick gray sweatpants. The outfit provided him with some bulk, and he didn't look as fragile as he usually did.

Delia and Randy were next, with Jacob trailing behind them in shorts and a sweatshirt. His hood was up, and his hands were in his pockets.

Therese and Tom came together, their first public outing. They were the same leathery bronze, but Tom was a good foot taller than her and at least twice as large. They sat down, looking embarrassed, and Tom put his arm around her. Therese looked younger somehow, and she was wearing a slight smile on her face. I wondered if, despite these macabre circumstances, this might nevertheless be was the beginning of her happiness.

It was chilly in camp that evening. I had jeans and a sweatshirt on for the first time since I'd been there. My flip-flops were dusty, and my toes were screaming for a pedicure. I combed through the knots in the underside of my hair while we waited.

If a stranger walked into camp they would have been very curious to know what we were all doing. Maybe they would have thought we were about to be pious and prayerful, or we were supporting each other in grief.

Luanne came running in and took a seat just before Detective Harris and Officer Carter made their entrance. She wore a fleece-lined zip-up jacket and shorts and was holding her usual mug of coffee.

I should have brought a glass of bourbon, I thought when I saw her mug. I considered running back to the cabin but decided it was too late.

Harris came in and stood in the center of the half moon of chairs. "Carter, how 'bout you build us a fire while I talk? You guys want a fire?"

He was so good. I wondered what he could have accomplished had he worked in New York City. On the other hand, his kind of charm probably wouldn't translate outside of the country.

Everyone nodded, and Carter put his scouting skills to work, stacking logs into the opening of the massive stone structure.

"I gotta tell you, this camp of yours is something else. People pay millions of dollars to have property with this kind of view. You've got a little utopia here, but you know that don't you?" He didn't wait for an answer. "It must have been very frustrating to have a woman like Emily English come in here and shake it all up. Emily. What a piece of work she was." He shook his head and looked around.

"You all seem like nice folks, and I gotta be honest, you didn't deserve what she was dishing out. Right? She was a blackmailer. You all know that. There are no secrets here. No, sir. That is something I've learned about you all." Harris shook his head and took a break from talking, walking back and forth slowly like he was thinking about what he had just said.

"No secrets," he repeated. "Emily, she thought there were some, but not between you guys. You all are as tight as family. She wanted in, and you wouldn't let her in, so she made you pay."

Everyone sat there taking it until Marge spoke up. "What are you getting at, Detective?"

"I'm getting there, ma'am. Just give me a minute here." He scratched his head as if it would help him remember where he left off. "I'll get to my point. I want to read something to you. It's from the New York State Penal Code. It states, 'Obstructing governmental administration in the second degree.'" He looked around the room for a reaction, but no one flinched. "A person is guilty of obstructing governmental administration when he intentionally obstructs, impairs, or perverts the administration of law or other governmental function or prevents or attempts to prevent a public servant from performing an official function...' I don't believe I need to keep reading. You may know the term Obstruction of Justice? It's a misdemeanor, for those of you who aren't aware. That could mean a year in jail. They don't have boats in jail." He ran his eyes over the group, watching for a response. Everyone sat perfectly still.

"I believe that the DA could prosecute each and every one of you for obstructing justice. I think maybe you've all lied to me or kept the truth from coming out. I like it here, don't get me wrong, but tonight we are going to get to the bottom of this so I can go home and sleep in my own bed. Carter here, he's a young man. He needs to be out living his life. He's not a security guard."

If Carter agreed, he didn't let on.

"I'm giving you one last chance to be honest with me if you haven't already. One—last—chance. This is it. You understand?"

Harris paused. "Now here is what I do know. I know that Emily was killed around nine forty-five on Tuesday evening. How do I know that? Because half a dozen of you saw Tom Johnson on the beach at his camp shortly before ten o'clock, and he and Therese Azzario had already seen Emily lying there on the dock…not that they did anything to help her!"

I looked around and was not surprised that no one let out even a small gasp of surprise. Marge sat up a little straighter, knowing she was next.

"Now don't go judging, because I think half the camp saw Emily lying there that night. Raise your hand if you saw Emily's body lying there on the dock that night. Come on, raise 'em. Last chance."

I looked around the room and saw Tom and Therese raise their hands, then Lester.

"I already know who else saw her, so maybe you need another minute?" Harris was looking directly at Marge, who raised her hand slowly and kept her eyes on the detective. Then he looked at Roz.

"I love that little boat of yours, Mrs. Martin. And you told me yourself you paddle every night if the weather allows. So why was the night of Emily's death different for you?"

Roz is a tough woman. She sat up a little straighter in her chair and looked him firmly in the eyes.

Before she could speak, Moe stood up. "Now listen here, I already told you she was with me!"

"You are weaving fairytales, Mr. Martin," Harris proclaimed. "Obstruction of Justice."

"Knock it off, Moe. Sit down," Roz said firmly.

Moe obeyed his wife.

"I did go out that night. I took my boat down to the dock, got one look at Emily lying there, and turned right back around," she said.

"Without checking for a pulse or calling for help?" Harris asked.

"Yes, sir," she said, still obstinate in posture.

"And why is that? Why would you not call for help?"

"Because I assumed she was dead." Her answer had anger behind it—a wall of cool granite anger.

"No, Mrs. Martin, it was because you were protecting someone else. I know it, and you know it. Now, when I think about what time that must've been, I figure it was right after you left the swim docks. You probably headed right into an argument down there. Who did you see arguing?"

She crossed her arms and stayed silent.

"Leave her alone. Please!" said a trembling voice. "Just leave Roz alone! It was me, okay? I killed her!"

"No, Jake! No! Sit down." Delia was pulling on his arm. "Sit down, please." She was crying, breaking my mother heart into a million pieces.

All eyes were on the boy as he stood there looking so alone. Maddy and Luanne were crying, I was crying, and poor strong Roz looked so destroyed. Moe was holding her as she hid her face in his chest. Jacob was the grandchild that she got to play with and cook for. The one that her own kids never brought. Randy was sitting with his hands against his face, rocking back and forth.

"I did it! I pushed her," Delia said, sobbing. "It was me! I pushed her. She was such a bitch!" she cried. "She deserved what she got."

"No you didn't, Dee. You don't have to lie for me," Jacob said, patting her head full of curls as he said it, consoling this woman who had given him so much love, who was his mother in every way except blood.

I sat there crying. My plan had worked, but with it came enormous sadness. It could have been one of my own boys in the same exact place. *It could have been them.* That's all I could think. I felt so responsible for that broken boy. I wished I could have saved him. I felt such shame. I'd done this. Me. I couldn't stand the thought of him carrying the burden of Emily's death around with him. I was sure that he would self-destruct if he had to live with it, so I did it for him.

I looked around the room thinking all eyes would be on me, but they weren't. How could they know this was my fault, that I had brought down a seventeen-year-old boy? Freddie was already walking back toward his cabin. *Had he known all along?* He'd advised me to be silent. Is this what he had meant?

Therese was wiping tears from her face, trying to put on a brave front. She knew Jacob from the quiet moments on the water. They'd sailed across the lake together in her tiny Sunfish until she'd taught him how to go it alone. He was one of her Lost Boys.

Lester was rocking in short back-and-forth motions, as if it helped him think through the events of the evening of Emily's death. I wondered if he felt guilty for not showing up earlier that evening. His sister patted his back and whispered something to him that I couldn't hear. He was her only concern.

Jack walked into the pavilion and looked around. "What the hell is going on in here?" he asked.

CHAPTER 36

ON THE NIGHT OF EMILY'S death, Jacob had been out wandering camp with the restlessness and boredom that came with his age. He'd nicked a pint of spiced rum that had been long forgotten in the cabinet of the bunkhouse and was almost finished with it when he bumped into to Emily on the lower dock. Until that moment, he hadn't even known he was angry with her.

He'd asked her not to take Roz or Therese's cabin. He told her that, if she agreed, he would convince Delia and Randy to switch rental cabins with her. But Emily wouldn't have it. Her acerbic response triggered a rum- and testosterone-fueled disaster that would change his life forever. He could barely remember the incident but said he could still hear the sound of her head hitting the dock. It had been haunting him.

Roz witnessed the entire thing. She sent him to his cabin and told him not to speak of it to anyone. She told him it would look like an accident.

When Randy and Delia got home that night, Jacob pretended to be asleep. Delia found him outside vomiting at two in the morning. He was crying and talking incoherently about killing someone on the dock. Delia had run out to see what he was talking about and found Emily lying there in a pool of her own blood. She assumed that Emily was dead.

In a clumsy rush to divert attention from Jacob, she grabbed a pair of Therese's flip-flops and walked through the blood. Then she rinsed the shoes in the lake, wiped them on a beach towel, and threw them back into the pile by Therese's doorstep. She fabricated a story about hearing someone on the trail that evening.

"I'm so sorry, Therese. I'm so sorry. I didn't know what to do. I'm so sorry," she cried to the tiny woman, who stood up and hugged her as they cried together for a boy that belonged to them both.

Delia insisted that Jacob tell Randy nothing. She knew he was incapable of hiding emotions and words. He was devastated by the news, continuing to rock back and forth in grief. Even Harris was heartbroken for him. The poor guy had lost so much already.

It was Roz who finally convinced Randy to go to the great room with Harris and Carter. "Your son needs you, Randy. Come on." She'd pulled him up by the arm and walked him out of the pavilion.

Harris had already told me that he would do what he could to convince the District Attorney that it had been an accident. Jacob was a minor and had been convinced by adults not to call for help. But those adults had aided and abetted in a cover up that they would be held accountable for.

We all sat there in shock for what seemed like forever after they'd walked Randy out. The fire was still burning when campers finally started to rise from their seats. Marge was leading Lester away. He seemed to be angry, and she was struggling to get him to go.

"Marge, hold up a minute!" I called out.

She turned and looked at me like I was a waiter she'd forgotten to tip.

"Don't think I've forgotten that you are responsible for Stan's death. If Luanne resigns, I am going to Parks to tell them what I know. Snapping turtles are protected in the park. Stan was innocent.

I will advocate for him and make sure you are prosecuted. The only thing that's kept me from doing it thus far has been Luanne."

"Are you blackmailing me?"

"I'm just stating the facts, Marge. You are free to decide what you want to do. But if she loses her job, I go to Parks," I said. "Oh, and the next time a Board position comes up, I'm going to take your advice and go for it," I said smiling. "I may even get into the lottery this year."

She huffed indignantly, and she and Lester headed down to their cabin.

I fell asleep in Jack's arms that night. The last words I remember him saying to me were, "You did the right thing."

I slept like I was dead and woke up late the next day. Camp was quiet, but I could hear sounds that indicated that life was going on; someone yelled from across the lake, a car door slammed, and birds were welcoming the day. Jack was gone, but there was a French press full of coffee sitting on the counter. I reheated it and poured it into a mug that said "#1 DAD." Then I walked down to the dock. Luanne was sitting in one of my chairs.

"I thought you were dead," she said flatly.

"That's all you need," I replied in the same tone.

"You just missed Jack. He's gettin' us breakfast at Earl's."

"God bless him," I sighed, sitting next to her.

"You got that right, sistah. The man's a saint. I know, I know, he's not perfect, but he's pretty damned close."

We sat quietly for a few moments.

"Thanks for everything, Lee. You saved my life. Really. I would have gone down for that murder. I don't know if Roz would have stepped forward to save me."

I turned around to see if anyone could hear her. Roz's cabin was just across from mine.

"They're gone. Left early this morning. Roz doesn't deal in emotion. She wasn't about to let anyone see how upset she was."

"She would have done the right thing in the end. I really believe that," I said.

"Marge and Lester are gone too. Up and out at dawn. I'll bet Marge was terrified she was going to be arrested for Stan's death," she laughed. "Can you imagine her in hand cuffs? The indignity," she said mimicking Marge. "I thought she was gonna crap herself when you said that yesterday. You think she's gonna say anything?"

"I don't know that it matters, Luanne. Maddy's on the Board. So are Roz and Therese. They aren't going to hold that against you. Have you heard anything about Bobby?" I asked.

"I called Sheila this morning. He's on life support." She shook her head. "Bobby and I have never seen eye to eye on things around here, but this is terrible."

I thought of the big bear of a man that I'd loved for years, lying there on a hospital bed unconscious, and all of his sins seemed to be forgiven. I started to cry.

"You ever comin' back here after this? Nice group a people, eh?" She put her arm around me and pulled me in.

"I can't believe the damage," I cried. "The camp is in ruins."

"Nah, camp will survive like it has for a hundred years. It's us that may not be here."

I wanted to tell Luanne that she should have been brave enough to come forward, but I didn't. I wanted to tell her that life is incredibly short and that her happiness could not wait. That it was urgent. But I knew she had to learn that lesson on her own.

EPILOGUE

◆ ◆ ◆

THOREAU SAID, "IF WE WILL be quiet and ready enough, we shall find compensation in every disappointment." It was time for me to be silent.

Jack took another week off of work, and we had our first vacation alone together in years. At night, we nipped away at a bottle of bourbon and played strip poker. One night we smoked a joint together, a rare occurrence, and slow danced to Ray LaMontagne in the tiny cabin, occasionally breaking loose to a faster song, laughing and spinning and coming up with goofy moves that made us buckle over with laughter. We paddled around the shore together sometimes and parted ways at others. One evening we slept under the stars on the very dock where Emily had died. It was a new beginning.

I spent my days surprisingly sober, swimming, doing yoga, reading, and taking long walks with Luanne. In the mornings, I worked on expanding my mediation from sixty seconds to five minutes, turning the tragic events of the past weeks into falling leaves.

New campers arrived, and by the following weekend, Club Montego was buzzing again with families and paddlers and those who had to see the dock where it had happened. It was time to go.

Jack and I told Detective Harris that we wanted to claim Emily's body. "She was a dear friend," I said to Harris with a wink. We would have her cremated and spread her ashes in the woods by the rock that I first met her on.

"I can testify to that," he'd said warmly.

On our last night, Red was loaded onto her rack, most of the cabin was packed, and Jack was getting his last paddle in. The sun had said its goodbyes, but I stayed on the dock in the last folding chair before it was loaded up in the car. Two beavers made their way past me, silent in the water. My heart was filled with gratitude at their presence.

One silent stroke at a time, Freddie appeared on the water. I hadn't seen him since the last meeting in the pavilion.

"Hello, Lee. It looks like you are enjoying this beautiful night."

"I am loving the silence, Freddie. Being as still as I know how to be."

"Good, good. I'm glad to hear it," he said, already pushing off again with his paddle.

"What did you know about that evening, Freddie? You were on the water. What did you see?"

"Millions of stars and the moon taking its shape back," he said.

I smiled as he drifted off silently.

THE END

If you liked this book, please review it on Amazon.com
or Goodreads.
It helps the author to get the word out.

Sign up at www.beth-everett.com for news, blog posts and
short stories

Follow on Facebook
fb/LeeHardingMysterySeries

Look for Lee Harding's third adventure, Where Charlotte Lay,
in Fall 2016

Acknowledgements

WITHOUT THE FAMILY OF SUPPORT I received while writing this book, it could never have happened.

Thanks to my husband Glenn for the endless confidence.

Jordan and Adrian, for listening even when they didn't want to.

My parents and my sister Cathy for always supporting my dreams.

Cassandra Longest, my sister in writing. I couldn't do it without you.

Deborah Kaplan, for being my guiding star in publishing.

Shannon Jamieson Vasquez, for her keen understanding of the subject.

Naomi Gamorra and Missy Jackson, for taking time out of their busy lives to mark up manuscripts.

Edel Rodriguez, you are pure genius.

Amanda Kruse, for combing through the details like the world's greatest detective.

Thanks to the members of the band Guster, for consistently making music that inspires, and for allowing me to use their lyrics without any red tape.

I'm grateful to my readers, Julie Fitzgerald, Megan Fielding, Sharon Sala, Vanesa Alcazar and Catrina DeVos. Thanks for the kindness.